Helen Brooks

RUTHLESS TYCOON, INNOCENT WIFE

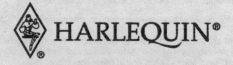

HARLEQUIN®

TORONTO • NEW YORK • LONDON
AMSTERDAM • PARIS • SYDNEY • HAMBURG
STOCKHOLM • ATHENS • TOKYO • MILAN • MADRID
PRAGUE • WARSAW • BUDAPEST • AUCKLAND

If you purchased this book without a cover you should be aware
that this book is stolen property. It was reported as "unsold and
destroyed" to the publisher, and neither the author nor the
publisher has received any payment for this "stripped book."

ISBN-13: 978-0-373-12781-8
ISBN-10:   0-373-12781-2

RUTHLESS TYCOON, INNOCENT WIFE

First North American Publication 2008.

Copyright © 2008 by Helen Brooks.

All rights reserved. Except for use in any review, the reproduction or
utilization of this work in whole or in part in any form by any electronic,
mechanical or other means, now known or hereafter invented, including
xerography, photocopying and recording, or in any information storage
or retrieval system, is forbidden without the written permission of the
publisher, Harlequin Enterprises Limited, 225 Duncan Mill Road,
Don Mills, Ontario, Canada M3B 3K9.

This is a work of fiction. Names, characters, places and incidents are
either the product of the author's imagination or are used fictitiously,
and any resemblance to actual persons, living or dead, business
establishments, events or locales is entirely coincidental.

This edition published by arrangement with Harlequin Books S.A.

® and TM are trademarks of the publisher. Trademarks indicated with
® are registered in the United States Patent and Trademark Office, the
Canadian Trade Marks Office and in other countries.

www.eHarlequin.com

Printed in U.S.A.

All about the author...
Helen Brooks

HELEN BROOKS was born and educated in Northampton, England. She met her husband at the age of sixteen and thirty-five years later the magic is still there. They have three lovely children and a menagerie of animals in the house! The children, friends and pets all keep the house buzzing and the food cupboards empty, but Helen wouldn't have it any other way.

Helen began writing in 1990 as she approached that milestone of a birthday—forty! She realized her two teenage ambitions (writing a novel and learning to drive) had been lost amid babies and family life, so she set about resurrecting them. Her first novel was accepted after one rewrite, and she passed her driving test (the former was a joy and the latter an unmitigated nightmare).

Helen is a committed Christian and fervent animal lover. She finds time is always at a premium, but somehow fits in walks in the countryside with her husband and old, faithful dog, meals out followed by the cinema or theater, reading, swimming and visiting with friends. She also enjoys sitting in her wonderfully therapeutic, rambling old garden in the sun with a glass of red wine (under the guise of resting while thinking, of course!).

Since becoming a full-time writer, Helen has found her occupation to be one of pure joy. She loves exploring what makes people tick, and finds the old adage "truth is stranger than fiction" to be absolutely true. She would love to hear from any readers, care of Harlequin Presents.

CHAPTER ONE

JUST a few more hours and then everyone would leave. She could do this; she had to. It was what her parents would have expected of her. She could almost hear her mother's voice—warm, faintly admonishing—saying, 'Come on, Annie, keep the flag flying high, sweetie-pie.' It had been one of her mother's favourite sayings when as a small child she had tried to duck out of anything unpleasant.

Marianne Carr drew in a deep breath and straightened her drooping shoulders. Checking her reflection in the bedroom mirror, she satisfied herself that the recent flood of tears didn't show and then left the room. On walking down the wide staircase she could see the odd person or two in the hall, but the main body of guests were in the drawing room. They were talking in the hushed tones one used at funeral receptions.

Crystal, her mother's housekeeper and friend who'd been one of the family for as long as Marianne could remember, met her at the foot of the stairs. Crystal's eyes were pink-rimmed and her voice wobbly when she said, 'Shall I tell them to come through to the dining room now? Everything's ready.'

Marianne nodded. She hugged Crystal for a moment, a catch in her voice as she murmured, 'You've been a tower of strength to me, Crystal. I couldn't have got through this without you.'

Crystal's plump chin trembled as she fought for control. 'I don't feel I have been. I still find it hard to believe they won't walk in the door, to be truthful.'

'I know. I feel the same.' It had been Crystal the police had notified the night of her parents' terrible car crash, two policemen calling at the house. Crystal had immediately phoned her and she had left her flat in London within minutes. On the journey back to Cornwall she had been in deep shock, praying the whole time that she wouldn't be too late. Crystal had told her her father had been pronounced dead at the scene of the accident but her mother was still clinging to life.

By the time she reached the hospital her mother had been able to tell the police that her father had collapsed at the wheel and the car had ploughed off the road, wrapping itself round a tree. She had had five precious minutes with the woman who had been her best friend as well as her mother. Five minutes to last the rest of her life.

The post-mortem had revealed that her father had suffered a massive heart attack and had probably been dead before the car had hit the tree. It was generally acknowledged it was the worst of luck that he had been driving at the time.

Forcing her thoughts into neutral, Marianne realised Crystal was dabbing her eyes again. 'I'll go and announce they can come through, Crystal. OK?'

'No, no. If you can hold it together, then so can I,' Crystal protested shakily. 'I'll do it.'

The two looked at each other for a long moment, drawing from each other's strength in the midst of their grief, and then Crystal bustled off.

Marianne glanced at her watch, a present from her parents for her twenty-first six years before. One o'clock. Hopefully the assembled family and friends would all be gone by four. She heard Tom Blackthorn's voice as she reached the drawing-room door and saw him standing with a tall dark man she'd vaguely noticed earlier. Tom was her father's solicitor and friend; he'd asked to stay behind after the others had gone so he could read her parents' will to her. She knew it wasn't just that, though. He would feel it his duty to point out that a huge rambling place like Seacrest was too much for a young woman to take on, that it would make more sense to sell it.

She wouldn't listen to him. She mentally nodded to the thought. Seacrest was in her blood. It had been in her father's, and his father before him. It had been her great-great-grandfather who had built the massive stone house on the top of the cliff over one hundred and fifty years ago, and Carrs had lived in Seacrest ever since. Although she had inherited it far too soon—her eyes darkened with pain—she would keep her beloved house going while she had breath in her body. It was part of her, part of her parents.

'Ah, Annie.' Tom had known her since she was a baby and, as he put out a fatherly arm and drew her into his side, she had to bite back the tears. To combat the weakness she kept her spine straight and her lips clamped together. 'I'd like you to meet the son of one of your father's old friends. Rafe Steed, Marianne Carr.'

Her inward battle to remain composed and in control in

spite of her grief during the funeral had rendered her almost blind and deaf throughout. Now, for the first time that day, she looked properly at the man she had noticed earlier at the church and then the graveside with Tom, seeing him as a person rather than another sombre-clothed shape among many sombre-clothed shapes.

The polite, How do you do? which had sprung to her lips was never voiced. He was tall—very tall—and broad with it. He wasn't smiling. Not that it was the time and place for smiles, she supposed, but there was something in the piercing blue eyes that was unnerving. After what seemed an endless moment, he said, 'Please accept the condolences of my father, Miss Carr. Ill health has prevented him making the journey from the States himself but he wanted to pay his respects.'

His voice ran over Marianne's overstretched nerves like icy water. It was deep, cold and liquid-smooth although the timbre was as hard as polished steel.

Mesmerised more by the coolness of his manner than his height and rugged good looks, Marianne said hesitantly, 'Thank you.'

She could not recall her father or mother speaking of anyone called Steed. Why had this old friend who lived on the other side of the ocean sent his son to represent him after all this time? It seemed strange. 'My father and yours were friends?' she said carefully. 'I'm sorry but I don't remember the name.'

'No reason why you should.' The big powerful body appeared relaxed but this did not detract from the energy and force it projected. 'My father and yours grew up together but my father left for America when he was in his early twenties.'

His accent was the type of lazy American drawl that was so attractive on the silver screen and even the lack of warmth couldn't negate its appeal. Marianne wondered why this stranger disliked her, because he did. It was in his manner, the set of his face and, most of all, his cold, cold eyes.

'I see.' She didn't but it didn't matter as the weight of her loss pressed down on her again. 'Please thank your father for me, won't you. I hope he is well soon.'

'My father is dying, Miss Carr, but slowly.'

The very sharply defined planes and angles of the masculine face showed no emotion as Marianne stared at him. She was completely taken aback but, before she could bring her mind to bear, Tom Blackthorn said, 'I'm sorry to hear that, Rafe. You didn't say before. We had some good times when we were younger—your father, Annie's and myself. The Three Musketeers.'

There was a small silence when Marianne wondered if Rafe Steed was going to ignore the man at his side, his eyes still intent on her face. Then, to her relief, the rapier gaze moved and he turned to Tom.

His smile wintry, he said, 'So I understand.'

What an objectionable individual. Marianne couldn't believe anyone would come to a funeral and then be so covertly rude to the bereaved. Drawing herself up to her full height of five feet six inches, which unfortunately was still almost a foot below the son of her father's old friend which, she felt, put her at something of a disadvantage, she said as coldly as he had spoken, 'Please excuse me, Mr Steed, but I have other people to talk to.' Nice people, *normal* people. 'I'll see you later, Uncle Tom.'

It had always been Uncle Tom and Aunt Gillian since

she was a child although they weren't related. Her mother and father had both been only children and so it had been Tom's two sons and two daughters she had looked on as cousins and, having no brothers and sisters herself, their friendship had been precious. It still was, although all but the youngest son had moved to other parts of the country.

As she made her way around the room, talking to one group of folk and then others, Marianne was uncomfortably aware of a pair of blue eyes watching her every move. Most people had plates of Crystal's delicious buffet in their hands by now but, although Tom had wandered off into the dining room, she knew Rafe Steed had not budged from his stance by the door.

'Who's the Heathcliff type Dad's been talking to?' As Marianne joined the group consisting of Tom's children and their partners and his wife, it was Victoria—Tom and Gillian's youngest daughter and the only child still unattached and fancy-free—who spoke. 'He's new round here, isn't he?'

'*Victoria.*'

As her mother shushed her, Victoria said, 'What? You know you want to know as well.' Turning to Marianne, she added, 'Dad just said he's an old friend but Mum doesn't know him and she thought she knew all of Dad's friends.'

Marianne smiled. Victoria was the maneater of the Blackthorn sisters. A confirmed bachelor girl with a fantastic career in central government, she had announced early in life that marriage and children weren't for her; neither were permanent relationships it would seem. It was common knowledge she ate men up and spat them out and, being a tall redhead with curves in all the right places and come-to-bed blue eyes, they queued up for the privilege of having their hearts broken. And Victoria had obviously set her sights on Rafe Steed. She was *so* welcome.

Keeping her voice light and easy, Marianne said, 'His *father* was an old friend, not him. Apparently your father and mine grew up with his. His name's Steed. Rafe Steed.'

'Steed?' Gillian was a Cornish lass, unlike Marianne's mother who had moved to the district from the north of England with her family when she was a young woman. 'He must be Andrew Steed's son. Yes, I can see it now although he's a head taller than his father was, but Andrew was very good-looking, too. They've got the same black hair and blue eyes. It was a combination that used to send the girls in a tizzwazz. With your father being so fair, Annie, and Andrew being so dark they used to have the girls throwing themselves at them.'

'What about Dad?' Victoria interjected a little defensively.

'Oh, your father was always mine,' Gillian said comfortably. 'Everyone knew that.'

Victoria's gaze was on Rafe Steed again. 'He's barely taken his eyes off you, Annie. And he's got a very sexy mouth,' she added, almost to herself. 'In fact he's "very" everything.'

'*Victoria.*'

This time her mother really meant it and Victoria recognised the tone. 'Sorry,' she said quickly to Marianne. 'I wasn't being flippant regarding your mum and dad, Annie. You know how much I thought of them.'

'It's fine.' It was. In fact, she preferred Victoria's naturalness to the awkwardness with which most people were treating her today. 'Why don't you go across and introduce yourself?' she suggested, knowing Victoria was longing to.

'You've got the excuse he's an old friend of your father's and, furthermore, he doesn't know anyone. You'll be taking pity on him.'

'That's just what I thought.' Delighted, Victoria was off.

'That girl.' Gillian shook her head while her two sons and eldest daughter and their respective spouses smiled indulgently. 'I don't know what it is about her but she attracts the men like bees to a honeypot. He'll be taking her out for dinner tonight, you mark my words.'

Marianne said something non-committal and moved on. She didn't care if Rafe Steed took half of Cornwall out for dinner tonight; she thought he was the rudest man she had ever met. If she saw him again in the whole of her life after today it would be too soon. Victoria was utterly welcome and, thinking about it, if anyone could bring such a man to heel, Victoria could.

She purposely didn't look over the other side of the room for some time, but when she did it was to see that Rafe Steed and Victoria had been joined by the rest of Tom's family and they were all chatting and smiling. Ridiculously, Marianne felt betrayed. The feeling disappeared almost as soon as it had come but it left her with stinging eyes and a trembling mouth. Suddenly she wanted her mother so much it hurt.

Don't be stupid, she told herself silently, walking across to the french windows and gazing out over the rolling grounds which stretched down to the high stone wall separating their property from the cliff path. She was a grown woman of twenty-seven and she had lived in London for the last five years since qualifying as an occupational therapist. She had a responsible job with a top London hospital and she had long since taken charge of her life. She was grown up, not a child.

It didn't help. Right at that moment she would have given everything she owned and was for five minutes with her parents.

You've still got Seacrest and Crystal. She hugged the thought to her as she fought back the tears. And, whatever it took, she would keep both. She would find a job down here and live at home and hopefully, if they were careful, she'd manage to pay the bills a large seven-bedroomed house like Seacrest produced. They could always do bed and breakfast in the holiday season; she'd been thinking about that in the last few days since the accident. And she would take care of the grounds herself rather than have the gardener her parents had employed one day a week.

If she had to, that was, she qualified, her eyes following a seagull as it swooped and soared in the blue June sky. She had no idea if there would be any money attached to her parents' estate; she and her parents had never talked of such things. There had been no need. Her parents had still been relatively young at fifty-seven and sixty respectively, and she'd had her flat and career in London. When she had come down to Cornwall for the occasional weekend or holiday, illness and death and wills had seemed as far away as the moon.

Eventually people began to take their leave. She knew the second Victoria and Rafe Steed began to walk towards her. Somehow she had been vitally aware of him the whole afternoon. She hadn't wanted to be—in fact, it had irritated and annoyed her—but somehow he had forced himself on to her psyche in a way which would have been humiliating should anyone have been able to read her mind.

'We're going, Annie.' Victoria enfolded her in a hug which was genuinely sympathetic. 'Call me as soon as you get back to the city and we'll do lunch. I don't know why we haven't thought of it before with both of us based in London.'

'Goodbye, Victoria.' Marianne hugged her back and then extracted herself to offer a polite hand to Rafe Steed. 'Goodbye, Mr Steed,' she said with deliberate formality. 'I hope you have a safe journey home and please give my best wishes to your father.'

He took her hand. 'I have some business to attend to before I return so I shan't be leaving for a few days, but I'll speak to my father before then and pass on your regards, Miss Carr.'

His flesh was warm and firm and, in spite of herself, Marianne became aware of the faint scent of his aftershave. There was the shadow of black stubble on the hard square chin and the expensive suit he wore sat with casual nonchalance on the big frame. He was a man who was comfortable with himself and his sexuality. *He would be dynamite in bed.*

The thought, coming from nowhere as it did, shocked Marianne into snatching her hand away in a manner that was less than tactful. For a moment they stared at each other, Rafe's features etched in granite and Marianne's eyes wide with confusion. Victoria, who had moved slightly to their left to say goodbye to her father, was thankfully unaware of what had transpired.

'Goodbye, Miss Carr.' It was expressionless, cold.

For a crazy, wild moment she wanted to ask him what she had done to make him dislike her the way he did. They had never met before this day; he knew nothing about her. She had thought at first he was probably the same with everyone, but he had been altogether different when he had been talking to Victoria and her family. Instead, she said, 'Goodbye,' and left it at that. She just wanted him to go now. She wanted everyone to go. But first there was the formality of the will. Once that was done—she took a silent gulp of air as she turned away from Rafe Steed—she could get on with sorting out her life and the changes she would have to make to avoid selling Seacrest.

Only it wasn't as simple as that.

An hour later, sitting across the coffee table in the drawing room from Tom, Marianne and Crystal stared in horror at the solicitor. 'I thought you knew.' Tom had said this twice in the last ten minutes since he had dropped his bombshell and his voice was wretched. 'I didn't imagine…I mean—' He stopped abruptly. 'Your father said he was going to tell you, Annie.'

'I suppose he was,' she said numbly. 'He'd asked me to come down to Seacrest the weekend before the crash but I'd got something on. I was coming down the next…' Her voice trailed away. 'How, Uncle Tom? How could he lose everything?'

'The business has been struggling for years but he hung on to the belief that the tide would turn. He thought borrowing against the house would be a short-term measure at first.' Tom waved his hands expressively. 'It wasn't. There's basically your father's boatyard and one other left in the area and that's one too many. They were both competing for a lucrative deal and they knew it would be the death knell for the one that didn't get it. The other boatyard won. It's as simple as that.'

None of this was simple. How could there be nothing

left? How could her father have risked losing Seacrest? Why hadn't he cut his losses with the boatyard and got an ordinary job somewhere? At least then Seacrest would have been saved.

As though Tom knew what she was thinking, he said quietly, 'The boatyard and Seacrest went together in your father's head, Annie. They were built at the same time by your great-great-grandfather—'

'No.' Her voice cracked. 'No, the house is different, Uncle Tom, and he should have seen that. Seacrest is…' She couldn't find the words to describe what Seacrest meant.

'There's no way at all we can keep it?' Crystal entered the conversation, her face white. 'I've got some savings, nearly twenty thousand in the bank. Would they come to some sort of an arrangement…?'

Her voice trailed away as Tom shook his head.

Marianne reached out her hand and grasped Crystal's. She would remember Crystal's offer all her life. 'What happens now?'

'The bank will claim what it sees as belonging to it, in essence. Then Seacrest will go on the open market. In the position it occupies and being such a fine old house, you'll be looking at a great deal of money. Even if you used Crystal's twenty thousand as a deposit, you wouldn't be able to make the mortgage repayments.'

'What if we did bed and breakfast, even evening meals, too? Turned Seacrest into a hotel?'

'Have you any idea of the cost of such a project? You'd need to do so much work before you could start taking guests. All sorts of safety procedures, not to mention converting the bedrooms into *en suites* and so on.'

'Three are already *en suites*.'

'Annie, we're talking tens of thousands to get the place round if you're going to get approval from the tourist boards and so on. Where's your collateral?'

'There has to be a way.' She stared at him, wild-eyed. 'I'm not going to give in. They can't take Seacrest.'

'Annie, to all extents and purposes it's theirs already.'

'Dad would have wanted me to fight this.'

Tom said nothing, looking at her with sad eyes as he laid out a host of papers on the table in front of her. 'Look at these overnight. This has been a shock, I see that, and if I had thought Gerald hadn't told you I would have said something before rather than dropping it on you like this. Take time to let it sink in.'

She didn't want it to sink in. She wanted Seacrest.

Somehow Marianne managed to pull herself together sufficiently to see Tom out and then comfort Crystal, who was beside herself. After Crystal's husband and two young sons of four and five had been drowned in a freak storm when he'd taken the boys out in his fishing boat, Gerald and Diane Carr had taken the broken woman in until she recovered sufficiently to decide what she wanted to do. Crystal's home had been rented and there had been no life assurance or anything of that nature. Shortly afterwards, the Carrs' housekeeper had suddenly upped and got married, and somehow Crystal had just taken over the role. That had been over thirty years ago and the arrangement had been a blessing for everyone concerned. Now, though, it was as though Crystal's world had ended for the second time in her life.

By the time Marianne had persuaded Crystal to go to bed

and taken the older woman a mug of hot, sweet milk and a couple of aspirin, she felt exhausted. Her head was spinning, she felt physically sick and stress was causing her temples to throb. Nevertheless, she sat down at the coffee table and began to work through the papers Tom had left for her.

There was no escaping the truth.

Tears streaming down her face, she opened the french windows and stepped into the garden, which was bathed in the mauve shadows of twilight. Immediately the scent from the hedge of China roses close to the house wafted in the warm breeze and, as she walked on in the violet dusk, pinks, sweet peas and honeysuckle competed for her attention, their fragrance filling the air. A blackbird was singing its heart out somewhere close, the pure notes hanging on the breeze, and far below the house she could hear the whisper of the sea on the rocks below the cliff.

This was her home. She had always known she would come back here one day. Boyfriends had come and gone and she had nearly had her heart broken once or twice, but deep inside she had always imagined coming back to the area she had grown up in, meeting someone local who would be able to love Seacrest like she did and settling down somewhere close. And then one day, when she was much older and her parents had had the joy of watching grandchildren grow up, she would inherit the house she loved with all her heart. And hold it in trust for her children…

Sinking down onto a sun-warmed bench which had retained the day's heat, she shut her eyes against the pain. If she lost Seacrest, then she would *really* lose her parents; that was how she felt. She couldn't explain it because of course they *were* gone, but here, in the house and garden which had nurtured so many generations of her family, she still felt close to them.

She sat on in the quiet of the night until it was quite dark, the leaves on the trees surrounding the grounds of Seacrest trembling slightly in the summer breeze. The moon had risen with silvery hauteur in the velvet-black sky, the stars twinkling in deference to their sovereign. It was a beautiful night. It was always a beautiful night at Seacrest, even in the midst of winter when harsh angry winds whistled over the vast cliffs, melancholy and haunting as they rattled the old windows and moaned down the chimneys.

Be it in the spring, when the swallows began to build their nests under the eaves; summer, when wild rabbits brought their babies onto the smooth lawns to eat grass that was sweeter than on the cliffs beyond Seacrest's boundary; autumn, when the trees were a blaze of colour and squirrels darted here and there anxiously burying nuts; or winter, when the sound of the sea crashing on the rocks filtered through shut windows and flavoured dreams, Seacrest was possessed of her own magic. The house was more than a house; it always had been.

She had to do something, but what? Marianne held her aching head in her hands, bewildered at how quickly her calm, happy life had been turned upside down. She didn't know which way to turn.

At midnight she walked back to the house, turning off the lights downstairs before retiring to her room. As she opened the door and looked at the room which had been hers as long as she could remember, desolation claimed her anew.

'Sleep.' She said the word out loud into the stillness. She needed to sleep and then she would be fresher to think of a way round this. This was the twenty-first century, an age of miracles when things were happening which would have been considered unthinkable a century before. It couldn't be beyond the wit of man—or woman in this case—to think of a way to keep Seacrest. She'd work twenty-four hours a day if necessary.

Stripping off her charcoal-grey dress, she threw it into a corner of the room. She would never wear it again. Nor the black shoes and jacket she had bought specially for the funeral.

Without bothering to brush her teeth or shower, she crawled into bed in her slip, an exhaustion that rendered her limbs like lead taking over. In contrast to the last few nights after Crystal's shocking telephone call, she was asleep as soon as her head touched the pillow.

CHAPTER TWO

OVER the next couple of days Marianne and Crystal followed one fruitless idea after another, but by the end of that time Marianne was forced to concede the situation looked hopeless. If either of them had shedloads of cash they could afford to pour into the old house it might be different, but if they had then they wouldn't be in the position they were anyway. Her father had gambled on the business reviving and he had lost. End of story, end of Seacrest. The debt was huge, colossal.

Marianne telephoned Tom Blackthorn on the third morning after the funeral. She and Crystal were sitting close together on one of the sofas in the drawing room, so they could both hear the conversation, their faces tight and strained. In a way it was even worse for Crystal than for her, Marianne silently reflected as she dialled Tom's number. At least she had her flat in London and her job to take her mind off things. Crystal had built her life around Seacrest and the family.

When Tom's secretary put her through, Marianne came straight to the point. 'I need to speak to you, Uncle Tom. It's no use burying my head in the sand and Crystal and I realise nothing can be done. How do things progress now? Am I allowed to keep any family belongings? Paintings and so on?'

There was a brief pause and then Tom said, 'I was going to phone you this morning, Annie. There's been a development we couldn't have foreseen.'

'What?' She glanced at Crystal, who stared back at her, eyes wide.

'I think it's better if I come and explain it in person.'

'Tell me.' There was no way she could calmly sit and wait for him to call. 'Please, Uncle Tom.'

'Someone's offered to pay the debts, lock, stock and barrel, so Seacrest doesn't go on the open market. Your idea of turning the house into a hotel would be part of the deal and this person would effectively expect to be a sleeping partner and receive fifty per cent of any profit once the hotel was up and running.'

Marianne blinked and kept her eyes on Crystal, who was looking as confused as she was. 'This person would buy Seacrest, then?' she asked numbly. 'It would belong to them?'

Again, there was a pause. 'Well, normally, yes, that's how it would be, but he's saying he wants only a fifty per cent ownership.'

'He'd own half and let me own half?' Marianne found herself floundering. 'I don't understand, Uncle Tom. Why would anyone do that? It doesn't make sense.'

'It's not unheard of for one partner to put up the capital for a venture and the other to take responsibility for all the hard work and the running of it, Annie. And it would all be legal and above board of course. I'd see to that.'

Her heart was beating so fast it was threatening to jump

into her throat. She could tell Crystal was feeling the same. 'Who is it?'

'I was instructed to put the proposition to you and see if you agreed before I make the client known.'

'Uncle Tom, it's me, Annie. Surely you can tell me?'

'I gave my word.'

Marianne sank back on the settee. Crystal looked as though she didn't know what day it was and hadn't said a word. Reaching out her hand, Marianne grasped the older woman's. 'What do you think?'

'Oh, Annie.' Crystal couldn't say any more—she was crying too hard—but she nodded vigorously through her tears.

Marianne tried to compose herself before she said, 'We're for it, Crystal and I. It would be daft to look a gift horse in the mouth.'

'I think so. This is the sort of break that comes only once in a lifetime.'

'And this person realises Crystal would be part of any venture?' Marianne asked. That was of vital importance.

'Oh, yes.'

'Then we'll do it. Who's the mysterious benefactor?' She'd been racking her brain for the last minute or two. She knew her father had had lots of good friends but most of them would find it difficult to raise the capital for a new car, let alone pay off a mountain of debt. It had to be a businessman in the town, one who'd known her father and who Tom trusted enough to listen to. That thought prompted Marianne to say, 'Did you approach this person or did they come to you?'

'It wasn't quite as straightforward as that.' There was

a pause and then Tom said, 'You remember Andrew Steed's son?'

Marianne's heart missed a beat. Not him. Anyone but him. He hadn't even tried to hide his dislike of her.

'He came to dinner last night and he was asking about you and so on. I'm afraid Gillian spoke out of turn and told him about the current situation.'

Oh, dear. Marianne could imagine how that had gone down with the solicitor. Her father's friend was one of the old school and he played everything absolutely by the book. A client's confidentiality was of paramount importance. She could imagine Gillian had received a lecture once they were alone.

'Anyway, it appears that Andrew owns a string of hotels in America which Rafe now manages. Over the last few years since Andrew's wife died and he became ill, he's been looking to return to the old country to end his days. Rafe's been in this area several times over the last twelve months apparently, looking for the right sort of place for his father. It's leukaemia,' he added.

'I'm sorry,' Marianne said mechanically.

'Anyway, apparently he has good patches and not so good, and it's not so good at the moment. Rafe feels his father's better when he is motivated. He always was something of an entrepreneur, was Andrew. He went to America with nothing and now it would seem he's an extremely wealthy man indeed. But I digress.'

Tom cleared his throat and Marianne waited.

'Rafe was concerned with this desire to return home to die. That was his terminology, I might add. Not mine. He did not feel it was altogether healthy and furthermore that it was out of character. Seacrest might be just the sort of tonic his father needs. He can take as large or as small a part in the proceedings as he feels able to, but Rafe would want you to make Andrew a part of it. Humour him, if necessary.'

'I see.' She glanced at Crystal, who nodded. 'I suppose that's fair.' They clearly didn't have any choice in the matter.

'Rafe was over here looking for a place for his father when he heard about the car crash from one of the locals. He told his father about it, who immediately wanted him to make himself known to you.'

'I see,' she said again, although she wasn't altogether sure she did. 'And has Rafe found somewhere for his father?' If this Andrew expected to stay at Seacrest she could see the project was going to be made more difficult with a very sick man to consider.

'Yes. A day before he heard about your parents' accident he put in an offer for the Haywards' place at the edge of the village. Made them an offer they couldn't refuse, apparently.'

Marianne knew the house, a great thatched whitewashed cottage with a dream of a garden. 'I didn't know the Haywards were thinking of moving.'

'There wasn't even time for a For Sale board to go up. When the estate agent contacted Rafe he offered an amount to seal the deal immediately, which knocked anyone else out of the water.' Tom's voice was wry when he added, 'I think he's a lot like his father.'

Oh, dear. In that case she wasn't going to like Andrew Steed one little bit.

'How about we do lunch today, the four of us? You and Crystal and me and Rafe Steed? Iron out any wrinkles before we commit ourselves properly. I want you to be completely happy about all of this, Annie. Your father would expect me to guard your interests as best I can. I've already informed Rafe Steed he will need another solicitor to represent him as you are my client.'

This was all happening so fast. Marianne swallowed hard. But what was the alternative to agreeing to Rafe Steed's amazing proposal? Losing everything, that was what. 'Lunch would be fine,' she said weakly.

'One o'clock in The Fiddler's Arms, then. To be honest, I'd like to get this sorted before Rafe changes his mind,' Tom said, and she could tell he wasn't joking.

When Marianne put down the telephone the two women stared blankly at each other for a second before Crystal gave a whoop and a holler that made Marianne jump out of her skin. 'I'll never say again there's not a Santa Claus. Who would have thought this could happen? It's unbelievable.'

Yes, it was a bit. Marianne let Crystal have her moment of joy but her main feeling was one of trepidation. It was a wildly generous offer and she was grateful to Rafe Steed—eternally grateful—but something didn't sit right. She didn't know what, but she'd bet her bottom dollar there was more to this than met the eye.

A little while later, as she walked up to her bedroom to get ready for the lunch date, she was no nearer to finding an answer for her inward unease. Whatever way she looked at this she couldn't lose, could she? It was a win-win situation. On one side of the scales she lost everything, on the other she kept a fifty per cent stake in Seacrest and in the future might even be able to buy the Steeds out if all went well. OK, it might take years, decades even, but it was a possibility and one she would work towards.

Opening the bedroom door, she walked over to the wardrobe. She needed to look businesslike, she told herself firmly. Cool and businesslike and in control. She always left a selection of clothes at Seacrest for holidays and weekends with her parents, but they were much less formal than her things in London. She must have something that would do. She glanced at the charcoal dress and black jacket, which were still where she had thrown them on the night of the funeral.

No. She couldn't bear to wear them again. Silly and emotional perhaps, but that was the way she felt.

The June day was a warm one, the sky blue and cloudless with just the slightest of breezes whispering over the garden and through the open window. Pulling out the most sombre dress in the wardrobe—a sleeveless sheer twisted tulle dress with attached dress underneath in pale brown—Marianne quickly divested herself of the jeans and vest top she was wearing.

Hair up or down? She surveyed herself critically. Up. More tidy and neat.

It only took a few seconds to loop her shoulder-length hair into a sleek shining knot, and she spent the remaining five minutes before she left the room applying careful make-up to hide the ravages a night spent crying had wreaked. True, her eyelids were still on the puffy side but only the most discerning eye would notice it.

By the time she joined Crystal, who was waiting for her in the hall, Marianne was satisfied that her overall persona was one of cool efficiency. Tom's last words, although spoken lightly, had hit a nerve. With salvation just a lunch away, she didn't want to blow this. She needed to instill in Rafe Steed the assurance that she could cope with whatever was necessary to get Seacrest up and working as a successful hotel.

'Annie. Crystal.' Tom stood up as they approached him and his companion in The Fiddler's Arms lounge bar, the tall dark figure at his side rising also.

Marianne kept her eyes trained on the middle-aged face in front of her until Tom had hugged her briefly. Then she forced herself to turn polite eyes to Rafe Steed. 'Hello, Mr Steed,' she said carefully. 'I didn't expect we would meet again so soon.'

'Likewise, Miss Carr.'

His voice was just as she remembered—silky, cold—but his face was as unrevealing as a blank canvas.

In spite of herself she was slightly taken aback and that annoyed her more than his coolness. She had expected... What had she expected? she asked herself silently. Some shred of warmth? Enthusiasm? *Something*, for sure.

Clearing her throat, Marianne said flatly, 'I appreciate the fact you might be interested in a business proposal involving Seacrest, Mr Steed.'

His eyes were very blue and very piercing. 'It's a little more than a might, Miss Carr.'

'Good, good,' Tom intervened, his voice brisk. 'But, in view of the circumstances, I think we can do away with such formality and move on to Christian names?'

Crystal nodded her agreement. Marianne's inclination of her head was less enthusiastic and Rafe Steed could have been set in granite. However, when he next spoke it was to Marianne that he said, 'I think our table is ready in the restaurant. Shall we?' and he took her arm in a manner that brooked no argument, leaving the other two to follow them as he walked her out of the lounge bar and through wide-open doors into the inn's restaurant.

Taken aback, Marianne didn't object but she was unnervingly conscious of the warm hand on her elbow and the height and breadth of him as he escorted her to a table for four in a secluded spot at the edge of the room. Once seated next to Crystal with the two men facing them across the table, she tried to relax her taut muscles but it was difficult. She didn't think she had ever felt so tense in all her life. Part of the problem was that she could feel Rafe's eyes moving over every inch of her face although she purposely hadn't glanced at him, pretending an interest in the room in general.

'So, Marianne…' He brought her eyes to his as he spoke, the deep voice with its smoky accent giving her name a charm she'd never heard before. 'What would you like to drink?'

'Drink?' She flushed as she realised she must sound vacant. Praying he hadn't noticed, she said quickly, 'A glass of wine would be nice.'

'Red or white?'

'Red.' Why had she said that? She never drank red. Was it because she felt he had expected her to say white? But that was ridiculous. He probably hadn't been thinking any such thing.

She watched as Rafe raised a hand and a waitress immediately appeared at his side. She had lunched at this particular pub many times in the past and she had never seen anyone get such prompt service before, not in the summer when the restaurant was always packed to bursting.

Once Rafe had given the order for drinks and they were settled with a menu in their hands, Marianne forced herself to raise her gaze as casually as though it wasn't taking all of her will-power and meet Rafe's eyes as she said, 'I understand you've bought the Haywards' place for your father. It's a beautiful old cottage, isn't it, and the garden is wonderful. I'm sure he'll love it.'

'I hope so.' It was flat, the tone contrary to the words. He swallowed some wine before he said, 'Personally, I think it is a mistake, this desire to come back to a country he left some four decades ago. All his friends and colleagues are in the States, that's where his life is.'

'What about his heart?' She hadn't meant to say it; the words had popped out of their own volition.

'His heart?' The blue eyes had iced over still more.

'Maybe his heart has never really left the area he was born in.' She paused for a moment. 'I could understand that, to be honest. I live and work in London, as you know, but I've always known I'd come back here one day to put down roots. Cornwall…well, it gets in the blood somehow. It can hold a person. But of course you would know your father far better than me,' she added hastily, sensing she was treading on thin ice.

'Quite.'

Oh, he definitely wasn't amused. She took in the tight line of his jaw and, as he cut the conversation by looking down at his menu, she noticed he had thick lashes for a man. Long and silky and curly—the sort of lashes a woman would kill for. His open-necked grey shirt showed the beginning of soft black chest hair and his broad shoulders accentuated the flagrant masculinity she had noticed the day of the funeral. She felt a little thrill in the pit of her stomach and hastily averted her eyes but for a moment the small neat words on the menu swam mistily.

Get a grip. She sat perfectly still for some moments, willing her racing heart to slow down. As her pulse gradually returned to normal she took a few discreet calming breaths.

Crystal, obviously sensing the tense atmosphere, dived in with the stock English fallback comment about the weather. 'Lovely for June, isn't it?' she said brightly. 'It was awful this time last year, one storm after another.'

Marianne raised her head in time to see Rafe's mouth twitch as he continued to keep his eyes on the menu. It annoyed her. He knew exactly how his attitude was affecting everyone, she thought irritably, and he didn't care. Possibly because he considered he was holding all the cards. Which he was, of course. Nevertheless... Expressionlessly, she said, 'Why haven't you bought Seacrest purely for yourself, Mr Steed? Or for your father, for that matter?' It was a question that had been burning in her mind since Tom had first told her about the proposal. She hadn't meant to put it so baldly originally but Rafe Steed had got under her skin.

Blue eyes met chocolate-brown and Marianne didn't try to hide the dislike she felt for this overbearing individual in her face. She felt Crystal squirm at her side and felt a moment's contrition. Crystal would be devastated if Rafe pulled out of this merger.

'I have a home in the States,' he said coolly after he had allowed one or two seconds to tick by. 'And Seacrest is too large an establishment for my father. The Haywards' place is much more suitable. But I think he will enjoy seeing it renovated and turned into a first-class exclusive hotel.'

Marianne's eyes narrowed. There had been something in his tone she couldn't put her finger on but which sent alarm bells ringing. 'As a project, you mean?' she said, a sudden tightness in her chest.

He gave her a hard look. 'What else?'

What else, indeed? Feeling as though she were wading through treacle and oblivious to the anxious glances the other two at the table were exchanging, she said, 'Correct me if I'm wrong, Mr Steed, but I felt there was something more to it than that when you just spoke.'

He settled back in his seat a fraction and the male face went blank, but she had seen the momentary surprise when she had pressed the challenge. Surprise and something else. She had been right; there was more to it than he had admitted thus far. Like a bolt of lightning, Marianne knew she had to get to the bottom of this. 'Am I right?' she asked directly.

He stared at her. It took all of her strength not to let her eyes fall away but she was determined not to be the one to look away first.

Tom began to say something into the taut silence which had fallen but in the next instant Rafe was on his feet, glancing at the other two as he said, 'I think Miss Carr and I need to talk privately for a few minutes. If you'll excuse us? We won't be long.'

'Annie?' Tom glanced at her, his face concerned.

'It's all right, Uncle Tom.' She had risen to her feet and now she smiled at the solicitor and Crystal. 'Order for us if the waitress returns, would you? I'll have the butter bean bruschetta with toasted wholegrain bread followed by the tarragon chicken with green beans and new potatoes.' She didn't think she'd be able to eat a thing but she was blowed if she was going to let Rafe Steed know that.

She glanced at him, waiting for him to express his choice, and for a second she thought she caught a glimpse of something which could have been admiration in the blue gaze. It was gone in an instant as he turned to Tom. 'The same.'

She didn't want him touching her again and so she quickly retraced her steps to the lounge bar. There she stopped long enough to glance over her shoulder and say, 'I suggest we go through to the garden. It's more private there,' before continuing on.

Once in the grounds of the inn she realised the tables and chairs scattered about the big lawn were full, which she hadn't expected. Normally, apart from the six weeks in July and August when the schoolchildren were on their summer vacation and even more holiday-makers flooded into the area, there was always a table or two to be had outside.

'My car's in the car park.'

Now Rafe did take her arm again; too late Marianne realised she should have been content with talking in the crowded lounge bar. The last thing she wanted was to sit in his car with him. Far too cosy.

As he led her out of the little side gate and into the large drystone-walled car park, Marianne was attacked by a number of conflicting emotions. His height and breadth made her feel very feminine, almost fragile, and it wasn't an unpleasant sensation. He smelled nice. Not so much the scent of aftershave but more the faint perfume of a lime or lemon soap on clean male skin—or perhaps it *was* after-shave? She didn't know but it was attractive. The set of his face told her she had been right in her suspicions that there was more to this than met the eye; furthermore, she wouldn't like what she was about to hear, and apprehension curled in her stomach. The sun was hot on her face and, as they reached a low silver sports car crouching in the far corner of the car park and he opened the passenger door, the smell of leather hit her nostrils.

Once she was seated he shut the door and walked round the bonnet of the car, sliding into the driver's seat as he said, 'I'm aware you have just lost your parents suddenly, which has been a great shock. If you would rather we had this conversation some other time that's fine.'

'Because I won't like what you say to me, Mr Steed?' Marianne asked steadily, refusing to be intimidated.

'Exactly.' He turned to face her, one arm along the back of her seat. 'And what I have to say doesn't alter the current proposal so it really isn't necessary to voice it.'

'I disagree.' Marianne folded her arms, wishing they weren't alone like this. 'I noticed at the funeral you had to force yourself to be civil to me and just now, when you mentioned Seacrest, there was something...' She swallowed hard. 'Perhaps you'd like to explain exactly how you feel?'

'Very well.'

It was said in a tone of *you asked for this* and Marianne's stomach turned over. Since she was a child she had always disliked confrontation but if and when it came she had invariably met it head-on.

'You know your father and mine grew up together, that they were boyhood friends?' said Rafe evenly.

'Yes.' Marianne nodded. 'Not until the funeral, though, but you already know that.'

'The three of them—your father, mine and Tom Blackthorn—were very close through their teenage years and then, when they turned twenty, something happened. Or someone.'

'I don't understand.' Marianne stared at him. He was speaking in a steady controlled voice but she knew he wasn't feeling calm inside.

'My father met a girl—a young woman. She'd recently moved to the area with her family. Your father and Tom had gone abroad for the summer—they had comfortably well-off parents, unlike my paternal grandparents, who were fisher-folk. My father's parents couldn't afford to send him to France and Italy to see the sights. He was expected to work on the fishing boat once he was home from university. They'd had to sacrifice much to allow him to go in the first place.'

He looked away from her, staring through the wind-screen. His profile might have been sculpted in granite. The clear forehead, the chiselled straight nose, the firm mouth and strong square jaw. He really was a very good-looking man, Marianne thought vaguely, but disturbing. Infinitely disturbing.

'The two of them fell in love, my father and this young woman. He was besotted by her. He couldn't believe such a beautiful young girl had fallen so madly for him. They had a wonderful summer together. She would wait each evening for him to return from fishing so they could be together. They had barbecues for two on the beach with the fish he'd caught, walks through the countryside, evenings sitting in the gardens of village pubs, things like that. She had golden-blond hair and the bluest of eyes, my father said. In that respect—the eyes—you are not like your mother.'

She had been expecting it, realisation dawning slowly as he had talked, but it was still a shock. Licking her lips, she said, 'Your father fell in love with my mother?'

'Not just fell in love with her—he always loved her. He still does. And my mother knew. She knew there was a girl in England he was trying to forget—a girl who had broken his heart and left only a small piece for anyone else. But my mother loved him enough to take what was left and make it work. They had a good marriage on the whole, even though she knew she was second-best.'

The bitterness in his voice broke through for a moment and Marianne watched as he took a deep breath, gritting his teeth. When he next spoke his voice was steady again, unemotional. 'Your father and Tom came back from their travels one week before the university term began. By the end of it your mother had switched her affections from the son of a poor fisherman to a man who had wealth and power in his family, the son of a successful businessman who owned a big fine house which would one day become his.'

Marianne's throat constricted. She cleared it, then said tightly, 'If you are insinuating my mother married my father for his wealth and property, you are wrong. They loved each other.'

He ignored this. 'The three of them—my father, yours and Tom—had one year left at university. On the eve of my father's graduation his father and brother were drowned in a storm and the fishing boat lost. My grandmother went to live with her widowed sister some miles inland. At the same time your father and mother got engaged. There was now nothing to hold my father here.

A mixed blessing in the circumstances. Certainly I don't think he could have stood seeing your parents settling into married bliss.'

She stared at him, colour burning in her cheeks and her hands clenched in her lap. How dared he say these things about her mother? How *dared* he? 'I don't know what went on all those years ago, Mr Steed, and neither do you, as it happens. You only have your father's side of things. But I do know my mother and she would never have done what you've suggested. If she cared for your father as you say I'm sure she was in turmoil when my father came on the scene and she realised what she felt for him was the sort of love that lasts a lifetime. Because that's what they had.'

'How nice and how fortunate it was the wealthy son of a businessman and not the poor fisherman who made her heart beat faster.'

He was doing it again—saying her mother had married for money. 'You're disgusting, do you know that?'

'Why? Because I'm telling you the truth?'

Marianne called him a name—one that made his eyes widen. 'It's not the truth, just your distorted version of it. I can't help it if your father is a bitter old man who has poisoned your mind as well as his.'

'Don't talk about my father like that.'

Marianne reared up at the hypocrisy, her voice flying up the scale. 'Your father? *Your father!* I'll say what I like after your insinuations about my mother. She was a wonderful woman, the best, and never in a million years would she have married my father simply because he was going to inherit a business and a big house. She wasn't like that.'

Her fury strangely seemed to calm him. His voice lower

than it had been a moment ago and without the growl to it, he said, 'Calm yourself, woman. You're overreacting.'

Marianne didn't think about what she did next; it was pure instinct. The sound of the slap echoed in the close confines of the car and immediately the handprint of her fingers were etched in red on his tanned face. She stared at him in the silence that had fallen, inwardly horrified at what she'd done but determined not to let him see it. She had never struck another person in her life.

Seconds ticked by. 'Feel better?' he drawled coldly.

She raised her chin. If she had tried to answer him she would have burst into tears and that was not an option.

'I can see we are going to have to agree to disagree about certain elements in the past.' He raised a hand to his face, flexing his jaw from side to side, one eyebrow raised. 'That taken as read, at least we now have all the cards on the table, so to speak.'

Marianne gathered herself together with some effort. Cards on the table? Hardly. If Rafe Steed and his father bore such an immense grudge about the past, then why the proposal regarding Seacrest? It didn't add up. Her voice as chilly as his had been, she said, 'Why are you and your father buying my home, Mr Steed?'

He made a show of relaxing back in his seat but Marianne was sure it was just that—a show. He was as tense as she was inwardly, she knew it.

His blue eyes narrowed against the sunlight streaming in through the window, he said quietly, 'I've told you why the offer has been made. My father and I are in the hotel business and have converted several suitable properties in the States. I think it would be healthy for him to have a project here rather than having to concentrate on his illness away from family and friends. He liked the idea of obtaining the house when I put the idea to him.'

'Because you both feel you're getting one over on my father?' she asked baldly, deliberately not mincing her words. 'Acquiring Seacrest would mean you'd secured the main thing which had persuaded my mother to marry my father, the way you see it, surely? Isn't that so?'

He surveyed her indolently for a moment or two. 'What a suspicious little mind you have, Miss Carr.'

'What a nasty little mind you have, Mr Steed.'

'I understand from Tom and Gillian that you are very like your mother.' It wasn't laudatory. 'In looks, personality—everything.'

'I hope so.' Her head was high and her eyes steady.

'She must have given the same appearance of fragility while being as—' he paused, obviously changing his mind about the next word before he continued '—strong as an ox beneath that delicate exterior.'

He had been going to say something unpleasant. Marianne's gaze never wavered as she said, 'My mother was a very strong woman, as it happens. She was also gentle and sympathetic and loving. You needn't take my word for that, ask anyone. But, on second thoughts, no, don't. It doesn't matter what you think. Not one iota.'

Hard-eyed, he said, 'And mine was equally loved, so how do you think it makes me feel, knowing she never had the marriage she should have had?'

'I don't know, Mr Steed. But that was your parents' business and no one else's, not even yours. From what you've told me, your mother married your father knowing about his past and how he felt so she knew where she stood. If they were unhappy—'

'I never said they were unhappy,' he interrupted brusquely. 'I think they were very happy in their own way.'

'But it didn't measure up to what you demanded they should feel about each other? They were supposed to have been the one and only loves in each other's lives, is that it?'

She watched as a veil came down over the blue eyes, making his gaze unreadable. 'There is no point in discussing this any further.'

She had never met a man who could get under her skin like this one. The arrogance—the sheer arrogance of thinking he could dismiss her after what he'd accused her mother of. 'I disagree. You started this and you can jolly well do me the courtesy of answering. And don't think you can hold the carrot of Seacrest dangling in front of my nose to make me agree black is white, because that won't work. I'd rather lose Seacrest completely than compromise on what I've said to you. Do you understand?'

He glared at her. 'Don't talk to me as though I were ten years old.'

'Then don't act like it.' She drew in a shuddering gasp of air, feeling as though someone had punched her in the solar plexus and desperately trying to firm her wobbly bottom lip. She would rather die than let him see how he'd devastated her.

She heard him swear softly under his breath and the next moment a large, crisp white handkerchief was placed in her hands. She reacted as though it were scalding-hot, shoving it back at him as she said, 'I'm perfectly all right, thank you.'

'Look, I didn't mean to say all that, but you're so...'

'So what?' Adrenaline was rushing in and it couldn't have been more welcome after the last few seconds of being in danger of losing control and bursting into tears. 'So like my mother? Well, I'll take that as a compliment if you don't mind.'

'For crying out loud!'

The irritation in his voice was acute and, as Marianne fixed her eyes on her hands, she willed herself to calm down. He was a pig of a man and she hated him, but what upset her most was the knowledge that she could never agree to the proposal to work with him and his father and keep Seacrest now. Desolation as deep as the Cornish sea claimed her and she sat in silent misery as she forced her racing heart to steady.

Rafe had jerked to face the dashboard, his hands gripping the steering wheel and his countenance as dark as thunder. Out of the corner of her eye, her gaze fell onto his hands. They were powerful and very masculine, his fingers long and strong and a light dusting of black hair coating the backs of his hands. He wore no rings but what looked like an extremely expensive watch sat on his left wrist. His nails were short and immaculately clean. She liked that in a man.

Hauling her thoughts back from the path they were following, she asked herself why on earth she was thinking about Rafe Steed's hands at a moment like this. Shock, most probably. The mind retreating into the mundane to cushion itself from the blow it had received. Not that there was anything mundane about Rafe Steed, she added with dark humour. That was one crime which could never be laid at his feet.

'To address your accusation about our motives for acquiring Seacrest, Miss Carr,' he said flatly after a little while. 'I plead not guilty, all right? And I know for a fact there was nothing of "getting one over on your father" in my father's motives for being interested in the property. He knew the house from a small boy and had spent many happy hours in its grounds playing with your father and Tom, added to which he was upset to find out that Diane's only child was to be turned out of her home. Genuinely upset. He is not a vindictive man, whatever you might think. It was as we were discussing the situation that the idea of acquiring Seacrest came to us. After all, Gillian had said something about you considering the possibility of a guest house.'

'That was when I didn't know about the debts and everything. I thought, at the worst, I had to pay for its upkeep and so on,' Marianne said numbly. She didn't know what to think about Andrew Steed's apparent pity for her. It rankled acutely that she would be beholden to someone who had maligned her parents so badly.

'My father and I thought of the partnership for practical reasons,' Rafe continued, as though he had sensed what she was feeling. 'I'm in the States most of the time and my father will not be in a position to contribute much physically to the alterations needed to set the hotel up and then the running of it once it's a viable proposition. We've found in the past it pays dividends if someone is on board who actually has a fondness for the property, who cares about it.'

In spite of herself, Marianne's interest was stirred. 'Are your hotels in the States converted old houses and that sort of thing, then?'

'Mostly, yes. We offer something different from the ultra-modern, chrome and glass establishments of the twenty-first century. Each of our properties are converted sympathetically. Some are large—eighty rooms or so—and others have merely a handful of rooms, as Seacrest will.'

He turned to face her again and she was conscious of the dark shadow of his chest hair under the thin cotton shirt he was wearing. Her mouth went dry. Ridiculous, but somehow her body kept insisting that she acknowledge her sexual awareness of this man when it was the last thing she wanted to do.

'I don't want to argue with you, Miss Carr,' he said flatly. 'I mean that. But I'm not prepared to let Seacrest go now my father has expressed an interest in acquiring the property. For that reason I shall buy the house, with or without you on board. If it helps your ultimate decision, most of my time will be spent seeing to our business in the States.'

Marianne flushed in spite of herself. She liked plain speaking but this man took it a step further. Nevertheless, it *did* help to know he wouldn't be around much. She had the feeling one male Steed would be quite enough to deal with, even if Rafe's father was an invalid. And if he was speaking truthfully when he'd declared their reasons for buying Seacrest—if it wasn't some twisted way to get even with her father—then she'd be crazy to refuse the offer. Once Seacrest had been converted into a small hotel and everything was running smoothly, she might be able to find another post as an occupational therapist down here and leave things more to Crystal. Anything was possible, after all.

She raised her eyes, to find Rafe giving her a long, searching look. 'The way I see it, my father was the injured party in all of this,' he said expressionlessly, 'although I appreciate you feel differently. I think he is being amazingly generous in honouring the memory of your mother by trying to help her daughter.'

'You think I'm ungrateful.' The antagonism which had begun to die down a little rose like a hot flood.

'In a nutshell.'

Charming. 'And I think you're rude and overbearing and narrow-minded.'

'Narrow-minded?' Rafe objected, raising his brows. 'Never.'

'Blinkered, then.' She wondered why he hadn't minded *rude and overbearing*. 'Seeing things only your way—the way your father has put them.'

'Excuse me for pointing out the obvious, but aren't you doing exactly the same?' Rafe said mildly. 'Seeing things purely from your mother and father's standpoint?'

Whilst mentally acknowledging he was right, Marianne said vehemently, 'That's different.'

'I thought it might be.'

Impossible man. Feeling outmanoeuvred, Marianne took refuge in cool dignity. 'I'm not prepared to discuss this any longer and I suggest if this deal goes through that ought to be the criteria for the future, too. On the rare occasions we meet,' she added crisply.

'Suits me.' His eyes had gone flat and cold.

'Good.' She looked at him and swallowed, feeling miserable. 'Shall we go back to the others now?'

'Of course.'

He had slid out of the low car and walked round to open her door for her while she was still fumbling with the handle, helping her out of the vehicle with the old-fashioned courtesy that was rare these days. But nice—very nice. Whilst being extremely capable and even fiercely independent on occasion, Marianne had never understood why some women objected to such little expressions of chivalry from a man.

They returned to the restaurant with nothing further being said and as they sat down at the table the waitress brought their first courses, which got them over an awkward moment. It was much later in the meal—over a wonderful dessert of pears poached in a rich citrus syrup—that Tom brought up the subject of the partnership. 'Do I take it any differences have been ironed out?' he asked carefully, and Rafe looked at her, one dark eyebrow quirked as he waited for her answer.

Marianne glanced from Rafe's dark face to Crystal's eager one and sighed inwardly. *I can't say no*, she thought with resignation. *It would be stupid. And he knows it. He knows he's got me over a barrel. And maybe I have seemed ungrateful thus far, but only because of his comments about my parents. And his attitude. Oh, yes, his attitude needles me all right.* Forcing a bright smile, she said, 'I think so. Mr Steed and I had a heart-to-heart and have agreed to disagree about certain issues which do not affect the proposal.'

'Right.' Tom appeared slightly anxious. 'Good, good.' He clearly wanted to ask what the issues were but didn't feel he could do so.

Crystal had no such inhibitions. Her expression changing, she leant forward and spoke directly to Marianne. 'Look, sweetheart, if you're not happy with something, then we'll think again, OK? What are these issues?'

'I'll explain later,' Marianne said in a voice which warned Crystal not to pursue it.

'That's settled, then,' Rafe spoke into the small silence which had fallen, his voice lazy and cool. 'I'll phone my father later on and, in the meantime, instruct my solicitor to have a word with you, Tom. We'd like to get this finalised quickly. I expect completion on the Haywards' property within two weeks and once my father is over here I see no reason to delay work on Seacrest.'

'Hang on a sec.' Marianne felt as if she'd been run over by a steamroller. Trying to control the host of emotions which had been rampaging through her head since their talk in the car park, she said, 'I've got to give in my notice at work and on my flat. There's loads to do.'

'Quite.' Piercing blue eyes bored into her face. 'Which is why delay is not an option.'

Sticking her heels in, Marianne glared at him. 'I have to give at least a month's notice at work.'

'In view of the unusual circumstances, I'm sure they would view things compassionately,' he said smoothly. 'Would you like me to have a word with someone?'

'No, I would not,' she said in a clipped voice. The very idea! 'I'm perfectly capable of saying anything which needs to be said, thank you, but there is no way I would leave them in the lurch by going early. I shan't be moving down here for a month.' She didn't add, *Take it or leave it*, but nevertheless the words hung in the air.

'Very well.'

Marianne stared into the dark face. She had won the first small confrontation, so why didn't it feel like it? Seconds later, she knew it was because she hadn't won.

'I shall therefore bring the selection of designs and ideas I've asked my architect to sketch out to you in London for discussion,' Rafe continued silkily. 'Until we've decided on the basics, work cannot commence. What's your address and work and home numbers? And your mobile number, too, please, in case I can't reach you any time.'

Marianne was lost for words. Here at Seacrest, she had Crystal to act as something of a buffer between them but in London there would be no one. She didn't want to entertain Rafe Steed in her small flat any more than she had wanted to sit in his car with him, but somehow that was going to happen. She gave him the required information stiffly, ignoring the glint in the blue eyes which told her more clearly than any words that he was thoroughly enjoying her discomfiture.

She managed to remain civil throughout the coffee stage of the lunch but by the time they left the restaurant she felt her nerves were stretched as tight as piano wire. The feeling wasn't helped when Rafe took her hand in the car park, shaking it and then holding her fingers a few seconds longer than was necessary when he said, 'Till we meet again in London, then.'

He was laughing at her. It didn't show in the expressionless carved features of his face, but his eyes were a giveaway.

Deciding her only course was to take his words at face value and pretend she didn't know, Marianne said carefully, 'Goodbye, Mr Steed.'

'I think if we're going to be partners we'd better drop the formality, don't you, Marianne?'

Again the sound of her name on his lips caused the traitorous shiver deep inside. Praying he hadn't sensed it, she said tightly, 'OK, fine,' and snatched her fingers back.

She was aware of his eyes boring into the small of her back as she and Crystal walked towards her little car, which was parked some way from his. It was only when they were inside and she had started the engine that she found herself breathing again.

'You all right, sweetheart?' Crystal asked quietly as Marianne swung the car round too fast and screeched past the two men without responding to Tom's raised hand.

'I'm fine.' *Fine.* The word mocked her. Would she ever be fine again for the length of time that man was in her life?

CHAPTER THREE

RAFE STEED watched the car drive away without responding to Tom's chatter at the side of him. In truth he didn't hear the other man, his mind and senses still tied up with the young woman who was the product of the marriage between his father's old love and his rival.

He had, quite unjustly, he admitted to himself, pictured a different kind of female from the one Marianne presented when his father had first told him about this love for Diane Carr. The fact that everyone had told him the daughter was the spitting image of her mother, both physically and in temperament, had prepared him for a cold, calculating, beautiful woman with her eye to the main chance. The sort of woman who didn't mind trampling over anyone who got in her way. He hadn't been too sure of Marianne's sincerity at the funeral—it was difficult to gauge the depth of someone at such an occasion, when emotions were naturally running high—but today she had surprised him.

'...hearing from your solicitor in the next day or two?'

Too late, Rafe realised Tom was waiting for an answer to a question he hadn't heard. 'Sorry?' He forced a smile. 'I was miles away, Tom.'

'I said I'll get things moving at my end straight away and I'll assume I'll be hearing from your solicitor soon.'

'Of course.' He nodded, wanting only to get away. 'Look, I've an appointment…'

'You go, Rafe.' Tom held out his hand and Rafe shook it. 'We'll talk soon.'

Rafe watched Tom drive out of the car park, raising his hand in farewell, but once the dust from the other man's car had settled he made no attempt to turn on the ignition of his hire car. He frowned and folded his arms, leaning back in the leather seat and shutting his eyes for a moment or two. He had been racing around like a headless chicken for the last week but it wasn't tiredness that was claiming his mind. He was used to living life in the fast lane; in fact, he thrived on it. He couldn't quite place what the feeling was that had him at sixes and sevens but it was all tied up with a certain woman with hair the colour of ripe corn and eyes like black velvet.

Damn it. He sat up straight, his eyes snapping open and his mouth hardening. What was the matter with him? He was too old and cynical to be taken in by a pretty face.

He watched as a young family came back to their aged saloon, the parents slightly harrassed as they ushered their three young children into the back of the car, settling the youngest one into a baby seat and making sure the seat belts were securely fastened round the other two. Those three children had no more than a fifty-fifty chance of their parents staying together long enough for the oldest to reach his teens, and maybe fifty-fifty was on the generous side. Monogamy, marriage, the promise *till death us do part* was a joke. As he knew only too well. But, having learnt the lesson, he wouldn't forget it. One venture down the aisle and a divorce which had been public and messy had ensured that.

Shifting irritably in his seat, he started the engine. Funny, but the kick in the teeth his failed marriage had given him hadn't seemed so bad as the recent revelations about his parents. He supposed that in a small part of his mind he had held them up as the perfect couple—proof that love could endure all things and remain constant to the end. Would he have preferred to remain in ignorance about Diane Carr and his father's feelings for another woman?

Damn right, he would. He drove out of the car park onto the Cornish lane beyond, the narrow road and high hedgerows limiting the speed of the sleek sports car. Ignorance really could be bliss after all.

Of course, thinking about it, he'd forced the issue with his father, by objecting to his move to England. It had been a mixture of desperation and exasperation which had prompted his father to tell him about his roots and his hankering for his homeland, along with the story of why he had left Cornwall and travelled halfway round the world in search of peace of mind.

And his father had found that with his mother—he knew that—but peace of mind wasn't enough. Rafe scowled to himself as he drove. However his father tried to explain it away by saying he wanted to end his days in the place where he had been born, close to his ancestors, it had been the memory of his first love which had driven him to come back. He knew it, whatever his father said to the contrary. Look how he'd been when he had first mentioned the girl being turned out of her home because of vast debts. Instead of his father taking hidden satisfaction in the turn around in his old rival's finances, he had been horrified for Diane's daughter.

His scowl deepening, Rafe changed gear with enough venom for the car to growl a protest. Well, one thing was for sure, once he'd got his father settled into the Haywards' place and the alterations to Seacrest were underway, he'd limit his visits to England to the bare minimum. His father had chosen the path he wanted the rest of his life to take and that was fine. Just fine. He didn't need his father any more than his father apparently needed him.

He reached a crossroads and waited for a pair of cyclists to pass in front of him, refusing to acknowledge the little voice in the back of his mind that was telling him he was acting like a spoilt brat. Once the cyclists had vanished in a jumble of long brown legs and brightly coloured shorts and trainers he continued to sit, the hot sunshine bouncing off the bonnet of the car and the haze of summer drifting through the open car window.

What was it about Marianne Carr that sent bolts of desire sizzling through his body every time he laid eyes on the woman? He didn't like it, he didn't want it and yet that day at the funeral—totally inappropriately, he admitted wryly—he'd been as hard as a rock from the moment he had first seen her. It was the last thing he had expected and it had knocked him for six.

A brightly coloured butterfly drifted in through one window and out through another as he continued to stare grimly ahead.

He was thirty-five years old, for crying out loud, and nothing if not a man of the world. He couldn't remember the last occasion a woman had affected him so primitively but it had been a long time ago, probably in his teens. There had been a cute little redhead in his last year of high school and she'd had every guy weak at the knees and uncomfortable in a certain part of their anatomy for an hour after she'd looked their way. Candy Price, that had been her name, and she had been built like one of the old Hollywood film stars, with curves in all the right places and eyes that promised paradise. Not that he'd found out whether that was true or not. Wealthy as his parents had been, she'd reserved her favours for Chuck Martin, the local millionaire's son, who had spots and braces but who drove a sports car and flashed the dollars around like money had gone out of fashion.

A toot behind him reminded him he wasn't the only car on the road and he pulled into the lane ahead, gathering speed as he drove.

But Candy Price wasn't at all like Marianne Carr. One was brazen voluptuousness and the other a cool-as-cucumber English miss who had a way of looking at you that indicated she thought you'd just crawled out from under a stone. Mind, she'd lost a little of that coolness today. His hand touched his cheek and he smiled darkly. He hadn't seen that slap coming but she sure packed a punch for such a slender young thing.

It had been his fault. He nodded to the thought. He could have put things more sensitively but somehow she had got under his skin.

No, be honest, he checked himself in the next breath. It had been the fact that he couldn't control the way his body reacted to her that had got under his skin, which wasn't the same thing. And, damn it, he didn't get it. He liked his women to be built on the lines of Candy Price rather than fragile and slender; women who were game for a lusty good time with no strings attached and who would remain friends once the affair was over. He was always honest, he always explained he wasn't the marrying kind—once bitten, twice shy—and that he would run a mile from commitment and everything that went with it. He'd found the world was full of beautiful, unattached women who saw life the same way he did. He had no complaints.

A bird suddenly flew from one side of the hedgerow to the other, narrowly missing the windscreen, and it was enough to jolt him into the realisation that the speedometer had crept up past seventy, which was far too fast for a Cornish country lane. Reducing his speed quickly, he told himself to concentrate. Ruthlessly wiping his mind clear, he continued to drive at a moderate speed, even humming quietly to himself after a while.

By the time he arrived at the little hotel where he was staying he felt calmer. It wasn't until he was in the shower later that evening that he realised he had come to some sort of a decision on the drive home that afternoon. He would give Victoria Blackthorn a ring, ask her out. She had made it plain she wanted to see him again when he had driven her home that day after the funeral and he had the feeling she would be on his wavelength completely. She was a very attractive young woman, feminine but independent and career-motivated. Just what he wanted, in fact. You knew where you stood with someone like Victoria, who had embraced equality between the sexes and had no compunction about letting a man know she liked him.

Towelling himself dry, he glanced at his reflection in the

mirror. As though it had argued with him, he muttered, 'OK, so there's something to be said for a man doing the pursuing, too, but not right now. Right now, Victoria is what I need.'

Even to himself he didn't sound convincing. Scowling, he flung the towel in a corner of the room and strode stark naked through to the bedroom, flinging himself on the bed and reaching for the TV remote. He *would* call Victoria but not tonight. Maybe when he took the architect's plans and ideas up to London he'd ring Tom's daughter and suggest dinner. For now he'd get room service to send up a bottle of Scotch and a steak; he couldn't be bothered to get dressed and go down to the restaurant. And his restlessness and irritability was nothing to do with the fact that he had behaved so appallingly to Marianne Carr and that she must hate his guts.

Flicking through the channels he settled on a twenty-four-hour news programme but almost immediately his mind went back to the matter in hand.

The last thing he would contemplate was getting involved with the daughter of his father's old flame; the woman was poison like her mother. She just hid it better. Whatever it was that had enticed the men in Diane Carr's day had been passed down in the genes, that much was clear.

He turned on his elbow and picked up the telephone. A few glasses of whisky and he'd reclaim his equilibrium. End of problem.

CHAPTER FOUR

'HE SAID *what*?' Crystal stared at Marianne, shaking her head. 'Look, I promise you it wasn't like that.'

'You know about it, then?' Marianne was beginning to feel as confused as Alice in Wonderland. Nothing was as it seemed. They were sitting in the drawing room at Seacrest with a tray of coffee in front of them, but she had succumbed to pressure from Crystal and related all that had passed between her and Rafe before she'd even had a sip of coffee. Now she reached forward and took a hefty gulp of the scalding-hot liquid before saying, 'Am I the only person in the world who doesn't know about Andrew Steed and my mother?'

'It was all so long ago, Annie. Of course I knew Andrew, having been born in the village about the same time as him, and when I first came to live with your mother she confided in me what had happened, but it wasn't general knowledge. She felt awful about hurting Andrew but the truth of it was, once she met your father she realised what she felt for Andrew was a pale reflection of the real thing. But Diane would never have been influenced by what either beau had materially. You must believe that.'

'I do. Of course I do.' But it didn't stop her feeling a little hurt that her mother had never told her about Rafe's father. Just for a moment Marianne understood a glimmer of what Rafe must have gone through when he'd found out. It was obvious he'd loved his mother and considered his father had short-changed her in some way, although from what she knew she didn't think that was fair. From all accounts, Andrew Steed had been completely honest with his American wife.

'I'm sorry Andrew's son is so hostile. I wondered why he was acting strangely, but it seems to me he needs to sort this out with his father first and foremost,' Crystal said firmly. 'He can't take it out on you just because his father loved your mother.'

'That's what I told him.'

'Good.' Crystal paused. 'He's rather dishy though, isn't he?'

'I hadn't noticed.' *Liar, liar, pants on fire.* 'Look, I've signed everything I can for the time being and I really think I ought to get back to London tomorrow and explain things to my boss and my landlord. Will you be all right here by yourself?'

'Of course. I'm used to holding the fort while your parents went on holiday or popped up to see you for the weekend, after all.'

'This is different, though,' Marianne said soberly.

'I'll be fine.' Crystal took a deep breath. 'I can begin sorting out the rooms and so on. We'll need to get organised if we're going to have builders tramping everywhere.'

'I'll come down again at the weekends but I feel duty bound to work out my notice.'

'Of course and you must.'

It was much later that night when sleep was far from her and she had tossed and turned and her bed was a tangle of sheets and duvet, that Marianne admitted she had been battling to keep Rafe out of her thoughts all day. It was humiliating—deeply so, in view of all he had said—but for some reason he had forced himself into her psyche and she couldn't get rid of him.

When the alarm clock on her bedside cabinet showed two o'clock Marianne gave up all thought of sleep and decided to go for a walk in the garden. She was hot and sticky and it would be cooler out there; it always was, with the sea breeze making itself felt even on the hottest summer night. Pulling her robe over her thin silk pyjamas, she thrust her feet into old flip-flops and left the bedroom, treading carefully so as not to wake Crystal, who was a light sleeper at the best of times.

Once outside, the cool night air was wonderfully fresh after the humid stickiness of the house. She breathed in its sweetness, scented with the rich perfume of roses and stock. Walking across the smooth green lawn which bordered the house, she wandered into the more dense blackness beyond, right down to the old gnarled seat which nestled in one corner of the large grounds close to the drystone wall. The trees which surrounded the gardens made the shadows pitch-dark but she felt no fear. This was her home, her sanctuary and she could never be frightened within its bounds.

Once seated, she felt for the little initials carved in the back of the seat. Her father had made the bench for her mother just after they were married and put their entwined initials in a love knot. It was too dark to see them but the feel of the little letters under her fingertips was comforting.

And then the tears came. In the house she had always tried to cry quietly, not wanting to upset Crystal, but tonight in the garden all restraint disappeared and she howled out her grief and pain and loss in a way she hadn't before. She was going to miss them so much and they had gone much too soon. It wasn't fair; none of this was fair.

She was in full flow when a sudden scrambling and disturbance on the other side of the seven-foot wall brought her heart into her mouth. She didn't have time to move before a voice said, 'Marianne, is that you? Don't be frightened. It's me, Rafe Steed.'

Rafe? Shuddering sobs were still shaking her frame as she desperately tried to recall what she had been moaning out loud. 'Mum' and 'Dad' had featured, she knew that, and she had been railing against fate.

The next moment a dark figure was on top of the wall. 'Can I come down?'

She couldn't believe this was happening. Her voice choked, she said, 'What are you doing here?'

'I couldn't sleep so I went for a walk on the beach. Then I decided to come back via the cliff path and I heard…' He paused. 'I thought about pretending I wasn't here but I couldn't. I'll go if you want.'

His voice was different; less cold, more…human. Marianne sniffed and inelegantly rubbed her nose on the sleeve of her robe in the darkness. She didn't know what to say.

The next moment he had settled the decision for her by dropping down into the garden. 'I can just see the gleam of your hair,' he began to say before going headlong.

She knew what he had tripped over. Her father had

bought her mother a little stone statue of a cherub one Christmas and positioned it near their bench. She heard him swear; the statue was shin height and, remarkably, considering the depth of her grief the moment before, she wanted to smile. She bet not many women had had the privilege of seeing Rafe Steed prostrate before them. Actually, neither had she. The darkness was too complete. 'Are you all right?' she managed after a second.

'I'll live.'

A moment later a solid shape plonked alongside her. She squeaked a little, she couldn't help it, before covering the involuntary admission of fright by saying quickly, 'You shouldn't be here.'

'Tell me about it.'

'I still don't see how you came to be outside Seacrest.'

'I told you, I couldn't sleep.'

Marianne's nostrils twitched. She could smell whisky on his breath. 'You've been drinking,' she accused. 'No wonder you couldn't sleep. Alcohol is a stimulant.'

'Spare me the biology lesson.'

Her nose was taking in something else, too—the clean, citrusy aroma that was part of him. Refusing to acknowledge how her stomach muscles had clenched, she said self-righteously, 'You shouldn't be walking on the cliff path if you're intoxicated, or the beach, come to that. And in the dark, too. That's foolhardy and dangerous.' Even to herself she sounded like someone treble her age.

Ignoring this, Rafe said, 'Are you feeling better now?'

'What?' Such was the power of his presence she had forgotten she had been crying. Recovering immediately, she said, 'Oh, yes—yes, thank you. It was just—Well, you know.'

'In part. My mother died five years ago but after a protracted illness. We had a while to come to terms with the fact she was going to leave us, although I don't know if that helped much when the time came. Anyway, I'm glad I've seen you.'

He was speaking as though they had bumped into each other out shopping or something and Marianne blinked in the darkness. She could just make out the outline of him now—big and dark against the sliver of moonlit sky slanting through the leafy branches of the trees.

'I was out of line earlier.' His voice was low and deep and smoky. 'Not that I spoke less than the truth, but it wasn't the time or place, not with the shock of the accident and all.'

'You might have spoken the truth as you see it but you're wrong.'

'I'm not going to argue, Marianne.' His tone said that was exactly what he was going to do. 'But the facts speak for themselves.'

She stood up. 'You've had too much to drink and earlier today agreed not to discuss this again. Come into the house and phone for a taxi. You shouldn't walk back to the hotel along the cliff path.'

He stood up, too, his voice impatient as he said, 'I've had a couple of whiskies, that's all.'

He was standing so close she could feel his body warmth reaching across the space between them and a tingle of excitement danced over her skin. The velvety darkness was perfumed with a thousand summer scents and the air was balmy and rich. 'It's gone two in the morning,' she said breathlessly. 'You shouldn't be here.'

'No, I shouldn't.'

He bent towards her and she did nothing to avoid him.
One hand closed around her wrist, drawing her into him,
and the other pressed into the small of her back, urging her
still closer. Marianne felt she couldn't breathe as she waited
for him to kiss her.

When his mouth closed over hers she felt the impact in
every part of her body, even though his lips were gentle, even
sweet. She had expected... She didn't know what she had
expected but his tenderness was her undoing. It cut through
any defences like a knife through butter and she found
herself wanting more as she pressed into him in a manner
which would have shocked her only seconds before.

'This is crazy.' His voice was husky against her mouth and
suddenly the tempo of the kiss changed, his lips becoming
more demanding as he sensed her response. 'Madness...'

She agreed with him but was powerless to move away.
The intimacy of the dark, quiet garden was like a different
world and, as she began to tremble, his lips moved over her
face with swift burning kisses before returning to her half-
open mouth. He plundered the undefended territory with
ruthless expertise and she heard herself moan as he triggered the desire for more. Her arms had wound round his
neck and her fingers tangled themselves in the dark crisp
hair at the base of his neck. He groaned in his throat and
at the same time she felt the unmistakable proof of his
arousal against the soft swell of her stomach.

It was all she needed to bring her back to reality and the
enormity of what she was doing. This was Rafe Steed—
Rafe Steed. The same man who had caused her such
anguish this afternoon and who had besmirched her
mother's good name, and here she was encouraging him

to think she was up for goodness knew what. Had she gone stark staring mad?

'No.' She struggled slightly against the broad chest and immediately found herself released. 'I don't want this.'

He didn't answer immediately but she could hear his ragged breathing as he stepped back a pace, giving her room. 'If it helps, neither do I,' he said after a long moment. 'It was a mistake, OK? Put it down to the whisky and the darkness and the general theme of knight in shining armour comforting fair maiden in distress.'

'Knights in shining armour don't behave like you've just done.' He had a cheek, calling her a mistake, Marianne thought furiously. And how dared he say he didn't want to kiss her?

'How many knights have you met to date?' Rafe drawled.

Unforgivably, the tone was one of amusement. Drawing on all her considerable will-power, Marianne forced any anger out of her voice and matched her tone to his. 'Not too many.' She could do the *this didn't matter a jot* scenario, too. She'd rather die than admit she was still trembling from the sensations his mouth and hands had wreaked.

'I'm sorry, Marianne. It won't happen again, OK?' His voice was cool and smooth now. 'I'm not usually so crass, believe me.'

She did. That kiss had told her Rafe was nothing if not experienced and supremely accomplished in the love-making department. Eternally thankful the darkness was hiding her flushed cheeks, she said lightly, 'Think nothing of it. I won't.' *And put that in your pipe and smoke it, Rafe Steed.* 'Now, do you want to come to the house and phone for a taxi?'

'No need. I told you, I only had a couple of whiskies. I'll continue my walk back if you're sure you are OK.'

'I'm fine.' *And I hope you fall off the path into the sea.* No—no, she didn't. But perhaps a twisted ankle or something similar would cause a dent in that infuriating self-confidence.

She saw the black bulk that was him move and then heard a scrambling noise, and when he next spoke his voice came from the top of the wall. 'I'll be in touch when I hear from my architect then. We want to progress things as quickly as we can so all this can be finished with.'

Quite. 'You've got my number in London,' she said coldly.

'Goodnight, Marianne.'

'Goodnight.' She heard him drop down on the other side of the wall and then the sound of his footsteps disappearing along the cliff path. 'And good riddance,' she whispered childishly, wrapping her arms round her middle as she shivered suddenly.

Once back in the house, she made herself a mug of hot chocolate for the comfort factor and carried it up to her room with a packet of chocolate digestive biscuits.

The mirror in the *en suite* bathroom showed a woman who had definitely been very thoroughly kissed. Her eyes were wide and dazed, her lips swollen and her cheeks burning. After splashing cold water on her face for a minute or two, she went and pigged out on the chocolate biscuits, eating the whole packet and finishing off with the mug of hot chocolate. It helped—a little. At four o'clock she had a long warm bath, generously doused with an expensive bath oil, and at five o'clock she packed for London and did her make-up.

Crystal was always an early riser and she looked up in

surprise from stirring porridge on the stove when Marianne strolled into the kitchen at six-thirty. 'I was going to wake you with a cup of tea shortly. I know you want to get away early. Sleep well?'

'Not the best night's sleep I've ever had.' Understatement of the year.

Crystal nodded sympathetically. 'It's all this with Rafe Steed, that doesn't help. Still, at least when his father's here he won't need to be around. We perhaps won't see him hardly at all after that. Tom says he's very much in charge in the States and it's a full-time job for anyone. Quite a little empire, apparently.'

Marianne nodded. She found she wanted to know more about Rafe Steed and yet she didn't, which made no sense at all.

'Did you know he's been married?' Crystal asked as she bustled about setting tea and toast in front of Marianne. 'Didn't last too long, apparently. Tom said he wouldn't talk about it, so goodness knows what went on.'

Married? She hadn't bargained for that. And divorced. Well, well, well. Perhaps that explained the cynical twist to his mouth. 'Poor woman, that's all I can say,' Marianne said flatly. 'Getting mixed up with someone as heartless as Rafe.'

'Well, we don't know he was to blame,' Crystal put in reasonably.

Marianne bit into a slice of toast, chewed and swallowed. Was she being unfair? Probably. Suddenly she didn't recognise herself any more and it was all his fault. Wretched man. Much as she loved Seacrest and Crystal and the area in which she had been born and brought up, she found herself wishing she could disappear back to

London for good. Something was telling her the next few months were not going to be easy in all sorts of ways.

He wanted his head examined. Rafe sat in the breakfast room of the small hotel he was staying in, staring moodily at his cup of coffee. How could he have been so monumentally stupid as to make his presence known to her last night? And, having done so, what had possessed him to further compound the error of judgement by kissing her? And not just a chaste comforting peck either; he could have got away with that and still retrieved something from what was a disaster.

His waitress arrived with his cooked breakfast. He glanced down at the plate and felt momentarily cheered. It was swimming with grease and the bacon had been frazzled to cinders, whereas the sausages still looked worryingly pink. Not much competition from this place then. If Seacrest couldn't do better than this they wouldn't deserve to pick up the custom. If there was one thing Steed hotels prided themselves on it was their attention to good food, be it an establishment sleeping twenty or two hundred.

Pushing the plate to one side, he buttered a slice of toast and spread it with a rather mediocre blackcurrant preserve, his thoughts returning to the problem which had given him a sleepless night. Marianne Carr. He didn't know what had drawn him to the beach below the house last night but that wouldn't have been so bad if he'd damn well stayed there. But, oh, no, he'd had to walk home via the cliff path.

Swigging the last of the coffee, he poured himself another cup. And once he'd heard her, what could he do but try to assist? He couldn't have just walked on. He wouldn't have left an animal in that state.

Face it, buddy. The voice in his head was relentless. *Since the first time you set eyes on the woman you have been fighting an overpowering need to take her in your arms and kiss her senseless.* And he didn't know why she fascinated him like she did. OK, she was lovely, but he knew lots of beautiful women and most of them didn't look at him as though he were the devil incarnate. Not that he could blame the present state of affairs on Marianne, he admitted irritably. He had set out to make sure she knew he had got the measure of her—and her mother—from their first meeting. No way was history going to repeat itself—that was what he had been determined on. His father might have been made a fool of by Diane Carr but he was a different kettle of fish. He knew what was what. He had learnt it a good while ago. Give a woman your heart and she would treat it like dirt, fit only to be trampled under her dainty little feet.

For a moment the image of Fiona, wrapped in the arms of her lover, flashed on the screen of his mind. It had been a good party, he had been enjoying himself until he had taken a walk in the host's garden to clear his head from the smoky, cloying air within the house. And he had fallen over them—literally. They had been too occupied in what they were doing to hear his approach and he had been thinking of his and Fiona's conversation in the car on the way to the party. He didn't want to put off having children any longer, he had insisted, and there was no reason for her to give up seeing her friends and having a social life—her normal excuse when he'd attempted to discuss having a family. He could work from home some of the time and share caring for their child and he was quite happy to hire a nanny, too.

It had been much later, in the midst of a divorce battle which had turned very ugly, that he'd discovered she had never intended to have children. She'd seen him as a meal ticket and an introduction into the wealthy golf and bridge set, and had been prepared to buy her place with her body and her lies. And he'd fallen for it, hook, line and sinker. The affair with the guy at the party had apparently been going on for some months and he hadn't been the first since their marriage six years before. Nevertheless, she had taken him to the cleaners without a shred of remorse. So much for women being the gentler sex. He smiled sourly.

But all that had been almost seven years ago. He had married at twenty-two and been divorced at twenty-nine, but since then he had made up for lost time. And he made no apology for it. Nor for the fact that he was not going to put himself in the position where betrayal could be an option again.

Reaching in his pocket, he drew out his mobile phone and punched in Victoria Blackthorn's number. No more walks on the beach. No more stolen moonlit kisses. He had his feet on the ground again. This brief…madness was terminated herewith.

CHAPTER FIVE

THE next week in London was hectic but Marianne welcomed this. She worked late every night at the hospital in an effort to begin setting the wheels in motion for an easy takeover by her replacement, who was yet to be appointed, making copious lists and notes to assist the new therapist. Once home, she ate her evening meal and then had an hour or so cleaning out cupboards and things of that nature before falling into bed about midnight. She wanted to leave the flat in pristine condition when she left.

As promised, she duly returned to Cornwall at the weekend to help Crystal with the heart-rending task of sorting out her parents' belongings and clothes. Most of these they packed away and put up in the roof space for the time being, neither of them being able to face actually disposing of them for the present. Thankfully, she saw nothing of Rafe Steed while she was home, but when she and Crystal accepted an invitation for Sunday lunch from Tom and his wife, Gillian mentioned that Rafe had taken Victoria to dinner in the previous week.

'I didn't know he was up in London.' Crystal turned to her. 'Did you see him?'

'Me? Of course not.' She kept her voice nonchalant, her smile untroubled. 'Why would I? He wouldn't have got the details from the architect yet.'

'No, I suppose not,' Crystal agreed, and then the conversation turned to Victoria and how well she was doing in her chosen career.

Marianne joined in and acted relaxed and interested, but inside there was a peculiar feeling which she couldn't put a name to. She didn't want to see Rafe Steed again, even though she knew it would happen, so why was she bothered that he had been in London and hadn't contacted her but had taken Victoria on a date?

But she wasn't, she assured herself silently in the next moment. Of course she wasn't. That wouldn't make sense. Nevertheless, she was glad when Sunday evening came and she drove back to London to begin another strenuous week which left her no time to think.

It was on the Wednesday evening and she had just got home from work and run herself a warm scented bath when her mobile phone rang about eight o'clock. One foot poised over the tub, she deliberated whether to ignore it and then bent down and rummaged in her handbag, which she had taken into the bathroom with her. These days, with Crystal all alone at Seacrest, she kept her phone by her night and day.

She didn't recognise the number. Even as she spoke, her heart began to hammer. 'Hello, this is Marianne Carr.'

'Hi, Marianne. It's Rafe.'

The deep voice was cool and smoky, the accent causing her toes to curl. She cleared her throat and then said carefully, 'Hello, Rafe. What can I do for you?'

'I've a few ideas I need to put past you. Have you eaten yet?'

'What?' Think quickly. Say yes. Simple.

'I've had a hell of a day and I'm starving. If you haven't eaten I thought we could thrash things out over dinner.'

Not like a date, then. And she was absolutely starving, having skipped lunch to fit an extra patient in. Cautiously, she said, 'A business dinner. Yes, that'd be fine. Where and when?'

'I'll call for you in say…fifteen minutes?'

'No need.' Distant and businesslike. She could do this. 'I'll meet you there, wherever there is.'

'Perhaps you could recommend somewhere? I'm still finding my way around.'

She'd bet Victoria chose somewhere glitzy-glam that cost a fortune. Mind, she would have paid very nicely for her dinner afterwards.

Horrified she could think such a thing and not knowing where the thought had come from, Marianne chose a steak house where the food was good, the service excellent and the whole was unpretentious. After agreeing to see Rafe there at eight-thirty, she stood staring at the phone in her hand for some seconds before coming back to life.

She had the quickest bath she'd had for a long time, washing her hair and then blow-drying it with one hand as she rifled through her wardrobe with the other, bringing out one garment after another and then discarding it until she had a pile a foot high on her bed.

What was she doing? At eight-twenty she caught hold of herself. This was not a date. This was so not a date. It didn't matter what she wore. Reaching for a pair of cream wide-legged linen trousers, she teamed it with a short-sleeved top in violet cashmere. It had rained earlier in the day and the evening had a slight bite to it. Slipping her feet into flat cream pumps, she ran a comb through her hair, which she left loose, and applied just a touch of mascara to her eyelashes. Finished. No titivating beyond a pair of silver hoops in her ears.

Grabbing a cream cardigan and her handbag, she left the flat at eight twenty-five. She had purposely chosen a restaurant that was a couple of minutes' walk away, and arrived dead on time.

Rafe was standing outside. He looked good. More than good. Much more.

He levered himself off the wall he'd been leaning against at her approach, smiling slightly. 'A woman who is punctual,' he drawled lazily. 'Are you real?'

'Very real,' she assured him evenly. Real enough to register it was time to admit he was the most attractive man she had ever met. Which would have given him an unfair advantage if it hadn't been for the fact that they disliked each other so thoroughly.

Once inside the restaurant they ordered steaks with all the trimmings and then sat facing each other over a bottle of red wine. 'So you've had a bad day?' Marianne asked politely. He looked tired. Perversely, it added to his appeal ten-fold.

Rafe shrugged. He had spent hours with the architect over the last few days but he still wasn't happy with what the man had proposed. The trouble was, he couldn't quite put his finger on what was wrong, which was unusual for him. He didn't like that, considering he thought indecisiveness one of the cardinal sins. 'I need to get back to the States,' he said quietly. 'I guess I'm getting impatient.'

She could imagine patience was not one of his virtues. The thought tilted her lips.

'What?' he asked, watching her.

'Nothing.'

'Come on.' He leant towards her, refusing to admit it was because he had caught the scent of her perfume outside the restaurant and wanted to smell the light but elusive blend that hinted of magnolias and warm summer nights again. 'Tell me.'

Marianne hesitated. She didn't want to start off on the wrong foot or it was going to be a long night with indigestion at the end of it. 'I wondered if you were normally impatient,' she prevaricated.

'Did you now?' He grinned, shifting in his seat and taking a long gulp of his wine before he said, 'There are those who would accuse me of that crime, yes. As I'm sure you can appreciate.' He leant back in his chair, surveying her from the piercing blue eyes that seemed to penetrate her mind. 'But we digress. I'd like you to take a look at these.' He pushed a folder towards her. 'Tell me what you think and don't be shy about giving your opinion.'

'About Seacrest? I won't.' Marianne opened the folder. Five minutes later, she said, 'I'm sorry, Rafe, but he hasn't caught what Seacrest is, what the house is about.' The intensity of what she was feeling caused her thoughts to tumble out in a rush as she went on. 'Seacrest can't be made into just a money-making enterprise. It deserves better than that. The alterations need to be planned by someone who appreciates that the house lives and breathes, that it has a soul of its own.' She stopped abruptly, a flush rising in her cheeks. 'Take the bar, for instance. It should be incorporated into the drawing room, unobtrusive but there to serve a need. And the dining room. Removing most of one wall so as to make it lighter and see the view is all very well but the house can't take that much glass. It's not right. And the extension to the present kitchen…' Her voice trailed away and he watched her struggling to find the words to express herself. 'It's practical and feasible but—'

'But what?' he asked quietly.

'But it's not what Seacrest is about. It should be on the left side of the house—a brand-new kitchen maybe, and the old one can become a small sitting room or a playroom for children. Seacrest could accommodate that.' She stopped abruptly. 'I don't suppose any of what I'm saying is making sense to you.'

'On the contrary.' He sat up straighter, the tiredness that had dogged him for the last hour or two gone. 'It makes perfect sense. And the extension on the right side of the house could take a couple of *en suite* bedrooms for people unable to climb stairs, perhaps? We could keep the extension a ground floor one but with a sloping roof and eaves, something that fits in with Seacrest's persona.'

Marianne stared at him. 'Yes,' she murmured. Ideal.

'So the proposed two-bedroomed flat for you and Crystal, do you still see that extending from the new kitchen?' Rafe asked, reaching forward and scanning the architect's sketch, which Marianne had laid on the table as she had begun to talk. 'Which would now be on the left side of the house.'

Marianne looked at the head of crisp black hair. He

wore it short—very short—and she suspected it had a tendency to curl. For an insane moment she wanted to run her hands through it.

She compressed her mouth, forcing herself to concentrate on the drawing. 'I think so, yes. It's more practical that way. Crystal is going to be chief cook and bottlewasher—that's her forte.'

'And you, Marianne? What's your forte?' he asked softly, suddenly raising his head and fixing her with his eyes. 'Tom tells me you work as an occupational therapist. Is that right? How will you adjust to such a radical change of career?'

'I don't see it like that,' she said stiffly. He'd hit a nerve. More and more over the last days, she had realised she didn't want to give up her work completely. It wasn't just that she had worked hard to qualify, although she had, but she loved her job, helping the patients to get back to active life after an illness or an accident, or helping them adapt with the minimum of heartache to any disability resulting from either. She enjoyed keeping the long-stay patients in hospital in touch with 'normal' life, trying to prevent them becoming institutionalised and dependent on hospital staff. Part of her work involved helping people to settle back into their homes and family after they had been in hospital, and suggesting and organising any necessary adaptations. Most of her patients became friends and she loved the fact that she could help in some small way for them to regain their self-confidence so they could plan for the future.

'How do you see it?' he asked quietly.

It was reasonable in the circumstances. After all, he and his father were investing an awful lot of money in Seacrest and they would want a good return. But she couldn't promise that she was going to be a full-time hotelier for ever. She took a moment to gather her thoughts. She had to be honest here. 'The work I do is very important to me,' she said slowly, wondering how she could get him to understand that it was more than a job—much more. 'And of course it's totally with people. I spend most of my time with the patients, gaining their confidence and trying to find out what their problems are and what activities might best help to solve them. No two people react to illness or disability in the same way so it's important to get to know the person really well and inevitably they become friends.' She raised her chin a little. 'I've found I'm quite good at making the right response to individual patients.'

He nodded. 'So you're saying what exactly?'

'I wouldn't want to give it up for ever. I could devote a couple of years to Seacrest full-time perhaps, but once everything is running smoothly I'd want to return to my work, even if it was just on a part-time basis to begin with. Before Mum and Dad died I was thinking—' She stopped abruptly. She hadn't meant to say so much.

'What were you thinking?' he asked curiously.

'It doesn't matter.'

His tone hardened. 'If it involves what you've just been talking about, I think it does matter.'

Again, she supposed this was reasonable. Marianne took a deep breath. She didn't quite know how they'd got on to this and she certainly hadn't meant to bare her heart to Rafe Steed of all people. But it was too late now. 'I seem to have a knack with children,' she said flatly. 'Some areas of a therapist's work can need extra-special training, particularly with children with congenital handicaps for instance, and I was thinking I'd like to specialise in this if possible.'

She raised her head and looked at him as the silence grew. His eyes were narrowed on her face and she couldn't quite read his expression but he wasn't pleased, that was for sure. Defensively now, she said, 'Of course this might not be possible now, I see that.'

Ignoring this, he continued to study her. 'Wouldn't that be…depressing? You're a young woman. Don't you want to have fun in your life?'

'Working with handicapped children and having fun in my life aren't necessarily incompatible,' Marianne said steadily, 'and you're wrong about it being depressing. It can be upsetting at times, of course it can, but the children are so brave and determined on the whole and without self-pity.'

Why was he pressing her when he didn't want to hear this? Becoming aware from her expression that he must be frowning, Rafe wiped his face clean of emotion. This woman was extracting herself from the neat little box in his mind labelled 'Marianne Carr' and it was unsettling.

He watched as the curtains of golden-blond hair swung either side of her flushed face as she bent to pick up her wineglass. Muscles clenched low in his stomach. Scented silk. Her hair, her skin—scented silk.

The kick from his manhood reminded him he was lusting after a woman who was undoubtedly not on the cards for him. If he believed her, and he found he did, she was too intense, too intelligent and too beautiful. Get involved with a woman like this one and you were asking for trouble, as his father had with Marianne's mother. He had been wet behind the ears when he had met Fiona and she had reeled him in like a fish. Looking back, he could see their relationship had been all about lust on his part and greed on hers. She had been shallow, a butterfly. Gorgeous to look at, but that was all. She had served as a salutary lesson in the wisdom of future autonomy, of taking what he wanted when he wanted it from women who knew the score and needed happy-ever-after as little as he did, but that was all. Fiona hadn't really left a deep ache in his life once he was over the initial sense of betrayal. This woman would be different. Like her mother, she had the ability to keep a man hooked long after she'd said goodbye.

'Anyway, you can rest assured I'll give one hundred per cent commitment until I'm not needed.'

Marianne's voice brought him back to himself. In a voice which sounded ungracious even to himself, Rafe said, 'Do I have your word on that?'

The deep brown of her eyes became like granite. 'I've said, haven't I?'

'Forgive me, but I've learnt not to rely on what a woman says.'

'Then you've been mixing with the wrong sort of women, Mr Steed.'

'We're past Mr Steed.' He grinned at her. 'You can insult me and still use Rafe, you know.'

He saw one corner of her delectable mouth twitch but she didn't smile, her voice prim as she said, 'I'll bear that in mind.'

The steaks came and were eaten, along with the dessert of chocolate fudge cake and ice cream. They talked of inconsequential things on the whole, keeping it light and informal, but Rafe found he was putting himself out to make her smile and then feeling inordinately pleased when he succeeded. Taking the warning the red light in his mind had flashed up, he ordered coffee for them both. He didn't think for a minute she would invite him in when he walked her home, but just in case…

Then he cut across all his good intentions by saying, 'So, anyone in your life at the moment, Marianne?' Cursing himself, he added quickly, 'I was just thinking it would be an added complication if so, with you moving to Cornwall.'

She seemed to take his words at face value. 'No one special,' she said lightly. 'I've lots of good friends in London but that's all. How about you?'

He shook his head. 'Long-term relationships aren't my thing—too difficult to maintain. The business comes first.'

She tucked a strand of hair behind her ear, the soft woolly top she had on clinging to her breasts. His body hardened.

'In a different sort of way, I suppose that's been a bit of a problem for me, too. My work involves unsocial hours at times, evening work visiting patients and families and so on, and there's always a mountain of paperwork to do at weekends.' She wrinkled her small nose. 'I ought to keep on top of it during the day at work but I find it more tempting to fit in an extra patient instead. Still, the reports and case conferences and all the rest of it have to be done. Not that I've lived as a nun the last few years, of course.'

She smiled at him and he forced a smile back. He found he didn't like the thought of her in another man's arms. Knowing he was opening a can of worms, he said, 'So you've never lived with anyone, been engaged, anything on that level?'

She stared at him for a moment. 'No.'

Knowing he had no right to ask, Rafe said, 'But you want marriage, kids, the whole caboodle at some point, surely?'

'Do I?'

She didn't seem offended, more amused if anything. 'Don't you?' he persisted evenly.

'Yes, I suppose so. Yes—' she seemed to make up her mind '—but everything would have to be right. I've seen so many of my friends settle for—' again she paused '—well, less than I would. I suppose it comes from seeing my parents so happy and in love.' She stopped abruptly, adding, 'Sorry, but they were.'

He inclined his head. 'Don't apologise. Mine were, too, in their own way.'

Uncomfortably now, she said, 'I wasn't trying to make a point, Rafe.'

'I know that.' He did. She wasn't the type of person to indulge in sly digs; she was too straightforward for that. Nevertheless, the more relaxed atmosphere of the last hour had vanished. He glanced at his watch and then stood up. 'I'll walk you home if you're ready.'

'No, there's no need for that. It's only a minute or two to my flat.' She stood up hastily, gathering her bag and cardigan as she said, 'Thank you for the meal. It was lovely.'

'I insist, Marianne. I've never yet let a woman walk home alone and I don't intend to start with you.'

'Rafe, this is a respectable part of London, not a no-go area in some foreign port or other. I'll be perfectly all right. I know the streets round here like the back of my hand and they are inhabited by nice respectable folk on the whole.'

He caught a shred of amusement in her voice and immediately his hackles rose. 'I'm walking you home,' he repeated tonelessly. 'That does not mean I intend to make a move on you, if that's what you're thinking.'

The amusement was gone when she responded vehemently, 'Of course I didn't think that. It's just not necessary, that's all.'

He didn't know whether to be offended or take it as a compliment. 'Necessary or not, that's what's happening.'

He kept his hand on her elbow as they walked to the door, the waitress who had served them—and to whom he had given a very generous tip—falling over herself to remind them that she hoped she would be seeing them again soon.

The air outside was cooler than it had been for some weeks and Marianne was glad she'd brought her cardigan. As she slipped it on, Rafe assisted her, his hand touching the soft skin at the base of her neck for a moment. It was a fleeting touch and without intent, but her skin burnt for some seconds from the contact.

They began to walk, passing couples sitting outside a pub enjoying a drink, then a few shops and business premises which were closed for the night before reaching a brightly lit jazz bar. Music drifted on the air from the open door and Rafe glanced in interestedly as they passed. 'Looks a nice place,' he murmured. 'Ever been in there?'

Marianne nodded. 'Once or twice. I like jazz.'

'Me, too.' It was on the tip of his tongue to suggest they might go together some time, but he restrained the impulse. It would send out the wrong signals. Not that he thought she'd agree anyway. She wasn't sexually indifferent to him—that kiss back at Seacrest had told him that—but

Marianne wasn't the sort of woman to be guided by her baser instincts. She would require mental and emotional fulfilment from a lover, not just physical stimulation. She would have to like a man, love him even, before she went to bed with him. Not the sort of woman he wanted to get involved with. Not in a million years.

They stopped outside a tall terraced house in a street full of identical properties. 'I'm home,' Marianne said brightly. 'And thanks again for a lovely meal. I'll wait for you to contact me about the alterations to the plans which we discussed, shall I?'

'Sure, I'll be in touch.' He cleared his throat. 'Was the landlord OK about you leaving? He wasn't difficult, was he?' What are you doing? he asked himself, aware he was making conversation in an effort to delay the moment of departure. Say goodnight and get the hell out of here.

'He's a she and, no, she was fine. She understood about Mum and Dad and couldn't have been nicer.'

'Good.' He stared down into her heart-shaped face. The breeze had wafted a strand or two of silky blond hair across her cheek. His hand reached out of its own accord and brushed the shining strands back into the sleek curtain. 'You must miss them a great deal,' he heard himself say.

He couldn't blame her for the surprise on her face. He watched as she hesitated, then said, 'Yes, I do. More as the days go by, actually, which is strange.'

'Not really. I think initially the mind is cushioned, especially in circumstances like yours when an accident's occurred and there was no warning.' OK, he told himself silently, you've done the comfort bit. Now leave. 'It's a process, grieving. You can't rush it.'

She nodded. 'Is that how it was for you? With your mother?'

'I guess so.' He didn't want to talk about his mother or his father or her parents. He wanted... Suddenly he cupped her face in his hands and kissed her hard before stepping back. 'Goodnight.'

He turned before she could respond, hearing her small 'Goodnight,' as he walked away. He had no idea if she was still standing there when he reached the corner of the street because he didn't allow himself to glance back.

CHAPTER SIX

MARIANNE saw and heard nothing of Rafe in the short while before she left London for good, and she was grateful for the respite. The evening she'd spent in his company and particularly the last minutes of it had unsettled her far more than she liked. She'd found she couldn't put him out of her mind for more than a few minutes at a time and it unnerved her. His kiss had unnerved her. Rafe unnerved her.

She had dealt with Rafe more easily when he was being obnoxious, she admitted to herself a day or two after their meal together. She hadn't wanted to enjoy being in his company but she had found herself doing just that. And his kiss. Why was it this man only had to touch her for bells to ring? It was humiliating, the response he triggered in her body with no effort on his part whatsoever. She was sure he had meant the kiss as a polite goodbye, that was all. Admittedly, an English person would have probably confined themselves to a peck on the cheek, but then Rafe was not English. He was American. And Americans were altogether less formal than their English cousins.

Thoughts like these continued to whirl in Marianne's head during the final days in London and the drive home to Seacrest. She had driven down to Cornwall the last couple of weekends, but now, with her bridges well and truly burnt behind her, this last journey felt different.

By the time she arrived at Seacrest with her personal belongings and suitcases filling every inch of space in her little Fiesta, she felt mentally, physically and emotionally exhausted. The weather didn't help. It had been raining on and off for days and the roads were wet and grey and misty.

After ascertaining that she and Crystal were seeing Tom the next day to go through some documents which needed her signature, Marianne pleaded a headache and went for a walk on the beach below the house to clear her head.

A wet shroud coated the landscape and it was unseasonably chilly. She spent a miserable hour or two wandering along the cold seashore, the sea mist turning the coastline a hazy grey and the small rock pools into slippy traps. There was the odd brave family on the beach, determined to make the most of their summer holiday whatever the weather, she supposed, but by the time she arrived home at teatime the sand was deserted.

She walked in like a drowned rat, water dripping from her coat and off her nose, and it was like that—with small pools of water at her feet—that she met Rafe in Seacrest's wood-panelled hall. He had just left the drawing room as she walked in through the front door and for a moment neither of them spoke.

Rafe recovered first. 'Damp out, is it?' he drawled with a magnificent lack of expression.

Marianne decided she couldn't win this one except by playing along, even if the piercing blue eyes were telling her she looked like something the cat would drag in. 'Just a trifle. Bracing, though.' She smiled sweetly, wishing him anywhere but here. And he would have to look totally drop dead gorgeous, without a hair out of place. Of course. 'I didn't see your car,' she added enquiringly.

'Came by taxi. I've been in the States for a couple of weeks and only just got back, I'm picking up a hire car tomorrow. I called by on the off chance you'd be around to discuss a few things. About—' he consulted the gold watch on one tanned wrist '—half an hour ago, and Crystal said you wouldn't be long and to wait. I've been eating her homemade fruit cake,' he added with schoolboy relish, 'and getting to know her a bit better.'

How cosy. And how very kind of Crystal to keep him here so he could witness her return. Through gritted teeth, Marianne said, 'If you'll excuse me, I'll just go and change before I join you.'

'No problem. I'm just on my way to the cloakroom.' As she made to pass him, he caught her arm. 'I've always wondered what a sea nymph might look like,' he said softly. 'Now I think I've got a good idea.'

Utterly taken aback, Marianne could only gape at him before recovering her aplomb enough to smile lightly and say, 'A sea nymph in a cagoule and wellington boots? I don't think so. I'll see you in a minute or two,' before scampering off to her room.

Once there, she stripped off her clothes, finding she was soaked right through to her bra and pants. After slipping into jeans and a warm jumper, she towel-dried her hair and pulled it up into a ponytail. She stood surveying herself in the full-length mirror, frowning slightly. What was it about Rafe Steed that made her overwhelmingly aware of his masculinity? It wasn't just his height and powerful build, although these were impressive, but there was a subtle kind of dark energy about him, a magnetism which was totally male and sensual. He was a disturbing man to be around and the more she got to know him the more disturbing he became. That last remark, for instance, about her looking like a sea nymph. A hundred men could have come out with something like that and she would have laughed in their faces, but not with Rafe. With Rafe she went weak at the knees.

Oh, for goodness' sake! The frown turned into a glare. This was crazy! If she didn't get a handle on this ridiculous feebleness it would become her Achilles heel, with the potential to make things more than a little awkward in the future. This venture was a business proposition, pure and simple. No time for girlish fancies. Too much was at stake.

By the time she entered the drawing room Marianne was composed and calm, outwardly at least. Crystal had lit a log fire—the damp sea mist could penetrate bricks and mortar on a day like this—and Rafe was sitting in a big easy armchair with an empty plate and mug at the side of him. He stood up at her entrance, smiling as he said, 'Crystal's in the kitchen making you a hot drink.'

Marianne nodded. Churlish of her, maybe, but he seemed to have taken over.

His smile vanishing and his voice flat, Rafe said quietly, 'I can leave if this is an inconvenient time.'

She stared at him, disliking how easily he seemed to read her thoughts. In spite of his polite words, she felt he knew exactly what she was thinking. 'Not at all.' She could be polite, too. 'I'm just a little tired, that's all. It's been a hectic few weeks.'

'I wanted to discuss a couple of things and I thought it would be easier face to face, that's all. But if you're too tired…'

'No, it's all right.' She made her way to the armchair opposite his and sat down.

'I'll get straight to the point.' He looked at her, his blue eyes unreadable. 'How do things sit with you financially? Oh, I know the situation regarding your parents' estate—' he flapped a dismissive hand '—but I mean now, over the next week or two until work progresses on Seacrest. Do you and Crystal have enough to live on?'

It was the last thing she had expected him to say. She blinked, taken aback.

Rafe almost smiled. Her face was like an open book. But he couldn't blame her for viewing him as a cross between Attila the Hun and the Marquis de Sade. He watched as she gathered her thoughts, the firelight dancing over her creamy skin.

'Thank you,' she said a little warily, 'but there's no need to trouble yourself on our account. I have some savings and so has Crystal.' A small smile touched her lips for a moment. 'We won't be begging on street corners for a crust of bread, not yet anyway.'

'Once everything is signed and sealed, an allowance will be made for your and Crystal's salaries. These will be paid directly into your accounts on the first day of each month. I trust this is acceptable? You can give Tom the relevant information when you meet him tomorrow—he's already liaising with my solicitor.'

Marianne nodded. Ridiculous and terribly unbusiness-like, but she had paid no thought to a salary of any kind, certainly not for herself at any rate. She had thought being a partner in the enterprise would be reward enough. But of course she would have to have something to live on and her savings wouldn't last for ever. 'There's…there's a lot more to all this than first meets the eye, isn't there?'

'Not really. At least not when you've done this sort of thing as many times as I have. Tom will acquaint you with progress to date tomorrow, but there's something else, something a little delicate.' He paused and then stood up abruptly, walking over to the full-length windows and standing with his back towards the room. It was raining in earnest now and twilight had come early, the room full of shadows which the flames of the fire caused to flicker gro-tesquely on the light-coloured walls.

Rafe's voice was low when he said, 'My father moved into his cottage today, Marianne. As I expected, the journey has taken a lot out of him and he's resting in bed. His housekeeper and her husband have come over with him—they've been with him for years, long before my mother died. They were going to stay indefinitely at one point but in the last couple of weeks they've discovered their only child, a daughter, is having a baby. Apparently, in the past, Jenny, the daughter, had been told she couldn't have children so Jenny and her husband, along with Mary and Will, are thrilled. The complication is that, due to medical reasons, Jenny is going to have to be confined to bed throughout the pregnancy and obviously Mary wants to be there to take care of her.'

He turned and looked at her. 'With anyone reasonable

this would not be a problem but my father is not reasonable. He's all for Mary and Will hotfooting it back to the States but refuses to concede that he needs someone living in permanently. He's insisting a daily and a part-time gardener will be sufficient. They most definitely will not.'

'I see.' She wrinkled her brow. 'No, I don't. What is it you're saying, exactly?'

'I need someone short-term to stand in for Mary—just until I can find a replacement—and I wondered if you would mind if I put it to Crystal? She's experienced and capable but, more than that, my father knew her when they were young. He's digging his heels in about having a stranger move in and he can be as stubborn as a mule when he wants to be.'

She rather thought it was a case of the pot calling the kettle black, but that wasn't her chief concern. How would she manage without Crystal? Until this very moment she hadn't realised how much the knowledge that Crystal would be at her side, supporting her, loving her, being there twenty-four hours a day had given her courage for the immediate future. It was necessary but she wasn't going to like seeing Seacrest torn apart and changed. It was going to be an emotional time, coming so shortly after the loss of her parents. Clearing her throat, she said flatly, 'Your father wouldn't manage with a daily and help outside?'

Rafe shook his head, rotated his shoulders and walked back to the chair he had vacated. Sitting down, he leant forward, his blue eyes piercing in a face that suddenly looked weary. 'He'd never forgive me for saying so, but he's ridiculously cavalier with his medication and so on. I know he resents being ill. This is the first time in his life he's ever had anything to do with doctors and hospitals and so on. He hates it. Hates the fact that some days he's as weak as a kitten. Other days he's more like himself and you wouldn't know anything was wrong.'

'You worry about him,' she said softly.

Rafe nodded, although his face gave nothing away. Ruefully, he said, 'He needs someone with him constantly to keep an eye on him, to make sure he eats properly, takes his pills, that kind of thing. Of course Crystal might not want to do it even if you agree.'

She wondered if he knew how effective it was—this big, rugged, hard man worrying about his father. It would melt the hardest heart. That aside, she had to admit that Andrew Steed probably needed Crystal far more than she did. 'You can put it to Crystal with my blessing and if she agrees I'll do what I can to support her as well as look after things here.'

He was very still for a moment and then sighed. 'Thank you,' he murmured, the powerful shoulders relaxing. 'He drives me crazy and half the time seems hell-bent on ruining what little health he has left, but…'

'He's your father,' Marianne put in quietly. 'I understand.'

'Yes, I think you probably do.' As though he couldn't help himself, his eyes dropped to her mouth, lingering there for a long moment.

Marianne sat still, her heart beginning to hammer in her ribcage. The atmosphere in the room had subtly changed, become heavy, languorous.

Rafe stood up and moved over to her, drawing her into his arms. 'Thank you,' he said again, his voice husky.

'You're welcome,' she whispered.

This time when he kissed her his lips were warm and persuasive, moving with a leisurely self-assurance that made her quiver deep inside. He was holding her close but she made no effort to try to move away because she didn't want to. She wanted him to go on kissing her. She had been waiting for this moment for the last three weeks, she realised with a little shock of surprise.

He raised his head for a moment, his hands moving to her ponytail. She felt his fingers loosen her hair so that it fell in a smooth, sleek curtain either side of her face.

'Beautiful,' he murmured thickly. As if drawn by an invisible silken cord, he lowered his mouth again and took her lips, her hair caught in his fingers.

Her hands slowly slid around his neck and he immediately deepened the kiss, slipping his tongue inside her mouth and exploring the inner sweetness. She didn't resist as his hands tightened in her hair, tilting her head back as his lips staked their claim, even though a small rational part of her mind was telling her this was madness. And it was madness, a sensual, magical madness against which she had no defence, never having felt like this before. Rafe was invoking sensations no other man had called forth and it was intoxicating. The warmth of his body surrounding her, the incredible things his mouth was doing to her—she didn't want it to stop.

'Marianne.' His voice was almost agonised against her mouth, his hunger naked, and it raced through her bloodstream, igniting nerve-endings and causing her to press closer into the hard male body.

The crackle and spit of a log as it fell deeper into the flames brought them apart, both thinking for a second that the door had opened and Crystal had entered the room. For a moment they stood still, bathed in the afterglow of sensation and sexual excitement, the only sound the rattle and hiss of the burning wood. Shadows danced across Rafe's taut face and she saw he was fighting for control. She wanted to reach out and touch him but she didn't. Something warned her not to.

'This is—' He stopped abruptly, shaking his head.

She waited, staring into the rugged handsome face without speaking. He didn't like the fact that he wanted her, she thought with a strange lurch inside her chest. Even more, perhaps, than she didn't like the fact she wanted him. But she did. Without rhyme or reason, against everything that was sensible and logical, she wanted Rafe to make love to her. She felt she was drowning in the sensations he'd aroused.

She watched as his inner torment turned the startlingly blue eyes to a deep violet. She could see sanity rearing its head as she watched him, the intimacy, which had been so real and soft seconds before, evaporating as he took charge of what he was feeling. It was a lesson in how self-disciplined he was, will-power and rigid strength of mind evident as his harsh breathing was subdued and his face became blank.

Before he could speak, she said, 'Don't say you're sorry or anything of that nature, Rafe, because we both know it was me as much as you.'

For a moment the mask slipped and his eyes widened.

'Let's just put this down as one of those things. It's clear we strike sparks off each other—sexually, that is. I suppose, with the tens of millions of people in the world, we're bound to come across someone at some time who can press all the right buttons.' She was talking nonsense but it was providing her with some degree of protection against the hot humiliation which had filled her as she'd watched him reject her. 'We know now, which will prevent us making the same mistake again.'

A corner of his mouth twisted in a wry smile which wasn't a smile at all. 'I'm a mistake?'

'Only as far as I'm concerned, and it works both ways,' she said steadily. She wasn't sure where the strength was coming from to talk like this but she blessed it.

Rafe's eyes narrowed. 'Meaning?'

'We're very different people and we want different things out of life. It would be a huge mistake to complicate what is essentially a business arrangement by getting involved.'

'Physically, you mean.'

She had meant romantically but if this wasn't confirmation that she was on a different planet from Rafe, nothing was. Or perhaps it was just the age-old complication of lust and… Her mind balked at the word *love* and substituted *intimacy*. By the nature of the act itself, men took and women received. The act of penetration was not the same emotionally for the two sexes, not in her book, at least. Drawing on her own considerable will-power, she said steadily, 'Exactly.'

A muscle knotted in Rafe's cheek. 'So you're saying this attraction is just a biological accident of some kind?'

'Yes, I am.' She stared at him. His eyes had gone as flat as his voice.

'Isn't that a little…cold-blooded?' he accused, his eyebrows raised.

'I don't think so,' she lied evenly. 'It's a well-known fact that animals respond to certain chemicals in their mates.'

'Excuse me, but I think I am a little more discerning than your average orangutan.'

Marianne smiled; she couldn't help it. He sounded so outraged. 'I'm sure you are.'

She watched him take a deep breath. 'You really are a very unusual woman, Marianne Carr.'

No, just one struggling to preserve the shreds of her dignity, she thought miserably. 'Thank you.' She forced a smile. 'I think.'

'And your parents?' he said softly. 'Did they have nothing more than this chemical response between them?'

'Of course not,' she said indignantly. 'They had masses in common, too, and they loved each other.'

'Ah, love.' He eyed her indolently, very much master of himself again. 'A complicated, elusive phenomenon and not one I would care to engage in.'

She was done pretending. 'You didn't love your wife when you married her?'

His eyes narrowed. 'My,' he drawled, 'what little bird has been whispering in your ear?'

'It's not a secret, is it?' She didn't lower her eyes from his in spite of the look on his face. 'You were married, you're now divorced. Hardly unusual in this age in which we live.'

'Possibly not, but when I married my wife I expected it to be for life. I had no wish then to add to the somewhat sad statistics of the twenty-first century and will take care not to in the future.'

That was all she was going to get; she could read it in

the cold blue gaze. And when Crystal chose that moment
to come bustling into the room, Marianne had never been
so glad to see someone in the whole of her life.

CHAPTER SEVEN

RAFE left the house twenty minutes later. Crystal had agreed she would consider the possibility of becoming temporary live-in housekeeper for a while for his father, but stressed this would depend on both Andrew's wishes in the matter and how she felt she would fit into the household when she met him again. She had also suggested the issue should be raised naturally in conversation rather than Rafe mentioning it beforehand. It was the best he was going to get and a great deal more than he had expected.

When the taxi he'd called dropped him outside the picturesque thatched cottage he didn't immediately go inside in spite of the drizzling rain. He stood in the shadows, cursing the fact he'd let his heart—no, not his heart, he corrected himself grimly, but a part of his anatomy situated somewhat lower—rule his head back there at Seacrest. It had been stupid and he was not a stupid man. Usually. Normally, having learnt a lesson once, he did not need to repeat it. And what he had learnt regarding the fairer sex was that they could be enjoyed, pampered, even worshipped as long as you took them at face value. You didn't trust women or expect anything from them and then you were not disappointed.

He pulled the collar of his jacket more tightly round his neck but still drops of rain trickled down his back.

Of course he hadn't given up on women, far from it. As a species they had a lot going for them and he thoroughly enjoyed sharing his bed and even his life with a beautiful woman for a while. But he always set out the rules of engagement before an affair began. When the time came for goodbye, as it inevitably would, it had to be quick and clean. No feminine manoeuvres, no bickering or name-calling, no regrets. He didn't want happy-ever-after and if a woman did, then regretfully he wasn't the man for her. Simple.

Why was he reminding himself of all this right now? And in the rain? One corner of his mouth twisted in a cynical smile. Because he'd let Marianne get under his skin, that was why. The thing was, she hadn't conformed to the mental image he'd had of her before he had come to England, apart from being lovely enough to addle a man's brains, that was.

Shaking himself, physically and mentally, he opened the front door of the cottage and walked into the hall. It was the very essence of a quaint English cottage. Because the previous owners had been emigrating to join their son and his family in Australia they had accepted an offer for all the furniture, which had been a bonus in the circumstances. Mary came bustling out of the door which led to the kitchen at the far end of the hall as he stood there taking off his jacket. She beckoned to him, motioning with a finger on her lips to remain silent.

'What's the matter now?' he asked as he stepped into

the kitchen, the aroma of fried chicken causing his nose to twitch appreciatively.

'Three guesses.' It was wry. 'He wouldn't stay in bed and he's insisting Will and I book our flights tomorrow.'

'He can insist all he wants.'

'I know that, Rafe, and of course we wouldn't dream of leaving him without a suitable replacement *in situ*, but you know what he's like when he's got the bit between his teeth. It's going to make things terribly difficult over the next little while till you find someone. *If* you find someone,' she added darkly. 'He's so against having a stranger in the house.'

'I just might have solved that problem.' Rafe's eyes went to the massive stove. 'When's dinner going to be ready?'

'Couple of minutes. Go through to the dining room. Your father and Will are already seated, but first—' she caught hold of his arm '—what do you mean, you've solved the problem?'

'*Might* have solved the problem.' Rafe swiftly put her in the picture.

'Oh, Rafe, that'd be marvellous. And this Crystal is coming round tomorrow?'

'She and Marianne together, on the pretext of meeting Dad and discussing business. Of course they might not hit it off. It's been half a lifetime since they knew each other and even then they weren't friends as such. But it's better than nothing.'

Mary nodded. 'Have you warned her how cantankerous he can be since he's got sick?'

Rafe grinned. 'Do you think I'm crazy? I want the woman to take the job.'

He left Mary chuckling to herself and made his way to the oak-beamed dining room, where he found his father having a pre-dinner drink with Mary's husband. The two men looked up as he entered the room and it struck Rafe how fit and healthy Will appeared compared to his father— one face tanned and bright-eyed and the other pale and washed-out. 'You took your time.' Andrew Steed scowled at the son who was his sun, moon and stars. 'I thought you said you'd be half an hour or so.'

'I was offered English tea, cake and muffins. How could I rush that?' Rafe said lightly. 'Marianne Carr's house-keeper does an incredible fruit cake. But of course you know her, don't you? Crystal Massey.'

Andrew nodded. 'It was Crystal Brownlow when we were at school, if I remember rightly.'

'Well, you'll be able to talk over your school days tomorrow. She's calling round with Marianne to discuss a few things regarding Seacrest.'

'Good.' Again Andrew inclined his head. 'I'd be inter-ested to see Diane and Gerald's daughter, but the sooner we get going on this project, the better. Time's money.'

It had been one of his father's favourite sayings regard-ing business in times past, but of late Rafe hadn't heard it. Now he noticed that, in spite of the exhausting journey his father had endured and the stress it had caused, his eyes were gleaming with the old enthusiasm he always dis-played at the start of a new venture. It boded well. Rafe took the drink Will had poured for him. It boded very well indeed. And if Crystal would just play ball tomorrow and his father would curb the stubborn streak which had got worse since his illness, the next little while might not be as difficult as he had thought. Only he, and maybe Mary and Will to some extent, knew how deeply depressed his father had become as his independence and self-sufficiency had been savaged by his illness. The doctors in the States had intimated that his father's state of mind could either make or break the treatment he was having, which had been one of the reasons he hadn't liked the thought of him being so far from family and friends. But perhaps—just perhaps—the move hadn't been such a bad thing after all.

Sunbeams danced off the mullioned windows of the old cottage as Marianne parked the car the next morning. In stark contrast to the day before, the morning was one of warm breezes and bright sunshine, the sort of weather that would have meant—had she been visiting her parents, as in the old days—a whole day on the beach just enjoying the sea, sand and sky. As it was... Marianne took a deep breath as she turned off the engine and smiled at Crystal. She had never felt so nervous in her life. Not only was she about to meet the man who could have been her father if her mother had felt differently all those years ago, but Rafe would be there, too. And, since that kiss yesterday, she hadn't known if she was on foot or horseback. And she couldn't share her confusion with anyone, which didn't help. Normally, Crystal would have been her confidante, but the older woman was too close to this situation.

'OK, sweetheart?' Crystal smiled back at her. 'Now, don't forget what I said. If you don't want me to take on the job of temporary housekeeper here until Rafe fixes a permanent solution, that's fine by me. You're my main concern. You know that, don't you?'

'Of course.' Marianne forced a brightness into her voice she was far from feeling. 'But if Rafe's father's halfway reasonable it would solve the immediate problem. Rafe was really concerned about him yesterday.'

Crystal's eyes were shrewd as she stared at the young woman who was like a daughter to her. 'You seem to be getting on better with him these days,' she said expressionlessly.

Marianne shrugged. 'Matter of having to, with us being business partners,' she prevaricated. 'Anything less would have made things untenable.' She opened the car door, effectively ending the conversation, and once on the pebbled drive said, 'What a beautiful place this is. I remember coming carol-singing here as a child and the Haywards were always very generous. They used to have everyone in for a hot drink and mince pies.'

Crystal didn't comment on the change of topic. 'They are a lovely couple,' she agreed, 'but they've been missing their son and his family like mad since they all emigrated a few years ago. It will be good for them to see their grandchildren on a day-to-day basis rather than once a year.'

Marianne glanced at her. She remembered her mother telling her the Haywards' son had been the same age as Crystal's eldest son and great friends with the boy. Crystal had had so much taken away from her by the sea, which had been the village's livelihood at one time, but she never seemed bitter or sorry for herself. Nevertheless, with the strong maternal streak she had, Crystal must have mourned the fact she would never have grandchildren of her own flesh and blood.

The thought caused her to reach out and hug the older woman briefly, saying, 'What would I do without you?'

'And me you.'

'So—' Marianne squared her shoulders '—let's go and meet Rafe's father.'

A nice smiley woman with a strong American accent ushered them through the sunlit hall and into a wood-beamed sitting room where Rafe and Andrew Steed rose to greet them. Marianne was immediately conscious of how similar the two men were, but also of how frail Andrew seemed beside the broad, vigorous figure of his son. Rafe introduced them and, as he did so, his father nodded his head, topped by a thick thatch of snow-white hair, saying, 'So you're Diane and Gerald's daughter. I would have known that without being told. I suppose lots of people have told you you're very like your mother, m'dear? But I can see Gerald, too. He had the same combination of fair hair and dark eyes. And Crystal—' he let go of Marianne's hand to shake Crystal's '—you haven't changed a bit.'

'Go on with you.' Crystal was laughing. 'I was a slim young thing in those days and my hair colour didn't come out of a bottle.'

'Come and sit down.' Rafe steered them to one of two sofas separated by a low, long coffee table, and he and his father sat down once they were seated. 'Mary's bringing coffee in a moment.'

Marianne tried very hard to appear as relaxed as the other three seemed to be but it was hard. She was glad Andrew Steed had mentioned her parents straight off but at the same time it had thrown her somewhat. She had expected... She didn't know what she'd expected, she admitted silently, but not this good-looking but gaunt elderly man with a rusty charm and eyes that were still a startling blue in the tired face. And he seemed nice. Not the rancorous, embittered person she had half been prepared to face.

She listened to the others talking, adding a word here and there when it was expected of her but otherwise trying to gain her composure. It didn't help her equilibrium one bit that Rafe was looking even more the brooding Heathcliff Victoria had labelled him all those weeks ago, his black jeans and black open-necked shirt sombre in the cream and gold room, and his tanned skin appearing even more dark against the light furnishings.

She plucked up courage to glance at him once or twice but it set the butterflies dancing madly in her stomach and dried her mouth. All in all, she was relieved when Mary appeared with the coffee. At least holding a cup and saucer gave her hands something to do. Thankfully, Crystal and Andrew were intent on going down memory lane, naming old school friends and incidents from the past that meant something to them.

Slowly Marianne began to relax. Andrew Steed wasn't the awkward, hostile individual she had feared he might be, and Rafe was polite but distant, very much the businessman. And she could handle that. It was the other side of him— the man beneath the outward persona—she had trouble with.

After coffee, Rafe spread the plans and drawings for Seacrest on the coffee table and they all peered at them, putting in the odd suggestion and discussing timetables and procedures.

At the end of an hour it was Crystal who, after glancing at Andrew's white face, said, 'I think we've all had enough to take in for today and Marianne and I have a lunch engagement in half an hour. Do thank your housekeeper for the lovely walnut cake, Andrew. It was delicious. You must be very pleased she has agreed to come over to England with you.' She stood up as she spoke, busying herself with slipping on her cardigan and not looking at him again.

Andrew irritably pushed Rafe's hand away when his son made a move to help him rise, standing up before he said to Crystal, 'Actually, Mary and Will are returning to America shortly.'

'That's a shame.' Crystal fluffed her hair, her voice nonchalant. 'Who will you have in their place, then?'

'A daily two or three times a week, if I can find one.'

'You'll be lucky round here.' Crystal tilted her head on one side, as though an idea was occurring. 'I tell you what, though, I might be able to help here. I'm going to be somewhat redundant at Seacrest while all the alterations are going on and I was dreading the brick dust and mess bringing on my dust allergy. If you don't get someone before Mary and Will leave, let me know and we could perhaps work something out.'

Andrew stared at her. 'But you couldn't leave Marianne.'

'Me?' Marianne took her cue from Crystal. 'Don't worry about me. I was worried about Crystal's allergy, to be honest. It can be a nightmare for her.'

'Really?' Andrew looked from one woman to the other.

'I was expecting to be hanging with my head out of the window most days,' said Crystal, warming to the theme. 'You'd be doing me a favour. But perhaps Mary and Will won't go.'

Andrew looked slightly sheepish. 'I booked their flight this morning, although they don't know that yet. They'll be leaving at the weekend.'

Rafe raised his eyes heavenwards behind his father's back.

'Well, think about it.' Crystal held out her hand. 'Goodbye for now, Andrew. It was nice meeting you again.'

'I'll see you out.' Rafe gently pushed his father back down into his chair and it said a lot about Andrew's exhaustion that he didn't object too much.

Once outside on the drive, Rafe said quietly, 'Thanks, Crystal. That was very tactfully done. I'm grateful. The thing is, he refuses to admit how sick he is and that's where the danger lies. If he's not kept an eye on, he'll do too much and then... Anyway, thanks again.'

'Any time,' said Crystal softly.

Rafe smiled at her and Marianne felt an ache in her heart. He had never looked at her the way he was looking at Crystal—openly and candidly. With her, there was always a watchfulness, even a wariness in his manner.

'You love him very much, don't you,' Crystal said softly, 'and that's natural, him being your father, but I can understand why he gets impatient sometimes. I remember him as one of those lads who was always on the go, never stopping for two minutes. Being forced to take things easy must be driving him mad.'

'You don't know the half.' It was rueful. 'He'd try the patience of a saint.'

'Well, I'm no saint, Rafe, so if I do come and stay for a while there'll probably be fireworks now and again.'

'Fireworks he can take, Crystal. It's boredom that's sapping his will.'

The blue eyes switched to Marianne and she felt the impact in every cell in her body. 'I want to thank you again for agreeing to let Crystal make the offer, however it works out. It was kind of you.'

Marianne flushed. It was a polite word of thanks but the wariness was there. 'No problem,' she said crisply, before swinging round and pressing the key to unlock her car.

Rafe followed them as they slid in, bending over and peering through Marianne's open door as he said, 'I shall be returning to America at the end of the week and it looks like I'm going to be tied up there for a month or so. I've let things slip a little lately, with all the visits to find Dad a place here and so on. I'd like to take you both out to dinner as a thank you for this morning before I go.'

'There's no need,' Marianne said quickly, 'and your father might not even agree to Crystal moving in for a while anyway.'

'Nevertheless, I'd like to take you both for a meal somewhere nice. Somewhere where you can dress up and take a breather from all that's been going on.'

Marianne opened her mouth to refuse again but, before she could voice the words hovering on her tongue, Crystal said, 'That would be very nice, Rafe, thank you. We'd like to come, wouldn't we, Annie.' It was a statement, not a question.

Marianne was tempted to tell them both to go together but, knowing Crystal would be upset, she said stiffly, 'Wouldn't you rather spend the time with your father if you're returning to the States?'

'I thought Dad might like to come along, too.' Laughing blue eyes took in her discomfiture. 'Unless you have any objection to that?' he murmured.

Marianne's flush deepened. 'Of course not.'

'Good, that's settled then. I'll be in touch tomorrow.'

'Fine.' She tried to ignore her view of his narrow-waisted, lean-hipped torso but it was hard. Thankfully, he closed the car door and straightened in the next moment and she could start the engine. Her last sight of him was in the rear-view mirror as she left the drive. He was standing with his hands thrust in his pockets, his black hair slightly tousled and falling in the merest of quiffs across his forehead. He looked so good that she functioned on automatic all the way home.

CHAPTER EIGHT

ANDREW STEED telephoned that evening to say he would be delighted if Crystal would stand in as his housekeeper until the work at Seacrest was finished, by which time he was sure he could arrange for a replacement to take over. While Crystal stayed with him Marianne must treat his house as her own, he added, and he would like to think she would come and share her meals with them both.

Marianne was glancing through colour schemes for the bedrooms, brochures spread out in front of her as she sat cross-legged on the drawing-room carpet, when Crystal finished the call.

'Come and have my meals with you and Andrew? I don't think that's practical,' she prevaricated when Crystal added her support to the suggestion. 'Maybe the odd evening meal but that's all. There's going to be heaps going on here I need to keep my eye on.'

'Exactly, and if you pop to us for lunch and dinner it's one less thing to think about,' Crystal stated, as though she were already in residence at the cottage. 'It'd put my mind at rest if nothing else.'

'I'll see how things work out.' It was a lie. She had no

intention of socialising with Andrew Steed more than was necessary. Not that she had anything against him personally now she had met him, although she still wasn't happy at his interpretation of why her mother had chosen her father over him. But perhaps that was more Rafe's view of the past rather than his father's? She would have to ask Andrew some time how he felt but that would be a good way into the future when she knew him better. *If* she got to know him better. Which she didn't really want to do because that would mean there was more likelihood of running into Rafe when he was over here visiting his father.

Her thoughts causing her head to whirl, she turned her attention back to the brochures. She wasn't going to let Rafe Steed dominate her mind, she was determined about that, she told herself firmly. And once this ridiculous 'thank you' meal was over she would make sure nothing similar happened again. Business lunches were one thing. Nights out on the town were something else.

What are you afraid of?

The thought came out of nowhere, as clear in her head as if someone had spoken out loud. Now she was no longer seeing the shiny leaflets and colour schemes in front of her, her eyes inward-looking.

Him. Rafe. I'm afraid of him. Not in a physical sense, because even in their few brief encounters he'd proven he was a man who was dangerously accomplished in the art of making love but who would stop the moment his partner gave the signal. No, it was a lot more subtle than that. For the first time in her life she had met a man who could potentially break her heart.

And then she caught at this last thought, telling herself

she was being silly. You had to love someone for them to break your heart and she did not love Rafe. She was sexually attracted to him but that was entirely different. She was just at sixes and sevens with herself over the loss of her parents and the huge changes in her life, that was all. She wasn't her normal logical, calm self. That was why thoughts of Rafe pierced her mind at the oddest moments and why she had a burning interest in who his wife had been, what she'd looked like, how they had met, what had finished the relationship.

Freudian theory would probably state that her brain was using Rafe as a diversion away from her grief. She smiled to herself. She could just imagine how Rafe would react if he was informed he was being used as a diversion for any reason whatsoever. Maybe she could do with a dose of psychoanalysis, grief counselling, call it what you would. Or perhaps she should simply buckle down to the job in front of her and put all her energies into that.

She nodded mentally. Yes, she liked that better than the thought of spilling out to a stranger. She had plenty of hard work and long days in front of her and that was exactly what she needed. At the end of this project, when she and Crystal were installed in their new flat and Seacrest was up and running as a successful hotel, Rafe Steed would barely feature on her horizon.

Rafe was very much on her horizon two nights later when she opened the door in answer to his knock. A taxi was gently purring away on the drive and Andrew raised a hand to her from the back seat, but all her attention was taken up with the tall dark man in the dinner jacket standing in front of her. Rafe looked… There weren't adequate words to describe how he looked, she told herself numbly, but if what he had could be bottled and sold it would make a fortune.

'Hi, there, all ready?' he murmured in his smoky American drawl. 'I can tell the cab to wait a while if you like.'

'No need.' She smiled brightly, as though her legs hadn't turned to jelly. 'Crystal is just checking everything's turned off in the kitchen. It's a ritual she does every time she leaves the house, although, to my knowledge, she has never left anything on by mistake in the last thirty-odd years.'

'There's always a first time,' said Crystal, coming up behind her, looking plump and pretty in a demure below-the-knee blue cocktail dress. Rafe was taking them to a very exclusive and expensive restaurant situated on the sea front in the next town ten miles away, where the small dance floor collected the rich and famous. The ocean-going yachts and boats moored in the floodlit harbour were always a sight in themselves. Needless to say, neither woman had been before but they had heard plenty about the clientele and not least the inordinately extravagant prices from the locals. It was definitely the sort of place for those fortunate individuals for whom money was no object.

'May I say every man is going to be green with envy when Dad and I walk in with you two on our arms,' Rafe said softly, his gaze moving over both women in turn.

'Thank you.' As Crystal echoed her thanks, too, Marianne was vitally aware of the forbidden turmoil inside her and eternally thankful Rafe couldn't read her mind. She was excited about this evening—who wouldn't be if they were being whisked off to the most sought-after establishment in Cornwall?—but dreading it, too. She wanted this one evening spent in his company in such wonderful surroundings with all her being, and yet she was terrified of it. But at least she felt she could hold her own with any other woman present. One of the female doctors at the hospital in London with whom she had been friendly had had the good fortune to have a sister who worked for one of the big fashion houses and—the two of them being a slender size eight—had been generous with any unwanted offerings. The draped and gathered copper cocktail dress strewn with pearls looked the part, there was no doubt about that, and she would even have paid the exorbitant cost it could have demanded for the boost of self-confidence in her appearance the beautiful gown had given her tonight.

Andrew had moved into the front seat of the taxi while the car had been parked, and when Marianne found herself between Crystal and Rafe in the back seat she tried very hard to ignore the feel of his hard thigh pressed against hers. It was difficult. Impossible, actually. She had never been so painfully aware of another human being's body in the whole of her life, and it was doubly ignominious that Rafe seemed totally unaffected in return. He chatted away easily, often leaning forward to make eye contact with Crystal and giving both women equal attention.

She could feel his strength and warmth through her thin dress every time he moved, and when he spread his arms along the back of the seat, his long legs stretched out in front of him, her senses went into hyperdrive. Her imagination running rampant, she was eternally thankful when the magnificent restaurant—a spectacle of chrome and glass and extravagant lighting—came into view. She had been able to make a pretence of joining in the conversation with some degree of normality—a private victory no one would appreciate but herself.

Rafe helped both women out of the car and then, as Crystal naturally paired with Andrew to walk in, Rafe took her hand and tucked it through his arm. 'You look like a million dollars,' he said softly. 'That colour suits you, you should wear it more often.'

'Thank you.' It was too soft, trembling. Terrified he would sense how she was feeling, she added more firmly, 'Have you been here before?'

'Once,' he murmured as they followed Andrew and Crystal into the glittering surroundings.

With Victoria? The dart of something hot caused her to mentally check her thoughts. Rafe could come here with whomever he pleased; he was a free agent, for goodness' sake.

And then she felt ashamed of jumping to conclusions when he added blandly, 'I was looking at a house in the area for Dad before the Haywards' property became available and called here for lunch. I promised myself I'd come back one evening and see the sun set in the bay. One of the waiters was telling me it's a magnificent sight.' He smiled, a sexy quirk of his firm lips. 'Of course, I thought it would be Dad and I on our own rather than having two beautiful women as our companions.'

Reeling from his smile, Marianne could only manage one of her own in response. And then she nearly died when he pulled her to a stop, the others a little way in front now, and turned her to face him within the relaxed circle of his arms. 'I want to say this now and it might help you to relax a little because you aren't, are you? Relaxed, I mean. And I can understand that. When we first met, I confess I was guilty of something I abhor in others—of prejudging someone. I'd decided you were... Well, something different from what you are. It doesn't excuse my behaviour, but I just want you to know I'd like us to be friends and not only because it will make things easier businesswise. I admire the way you've turned your life round without a word of self-pity and without collapsing under the pressure. OK?'

She stared at him. Her addled brain had taken in the gist of what he was saying but the word *friends* had stood out. It was a nice apology for the way he had treated her initially, she thought, and now she had got to know him a little she knew he wouldn't have voiced it unless he'd really meant it, but at the same time he was making the point that it was friendship and nothing else he was offering. She made a Herculean effort at normality and said with admirable composure, 'I can understand how you were feeling, Rafe. Finding out about your father's reason for leaving England must have been a shock. I found it difficult enough when you told me. Let's forget about everything thus far, shall we? And, yes, I'd like to be friends, even though I suspect we'll have to agree to disagree about certain things because we are very different people. But that doesn't matter with friends.'

He opened his mouth to say something but, before he could speak, Andrew's voice bellowed irritably, 'Come on, you two.'

Using Rafe's father as an excuse, Marianne seized the moment to slip out of Rafe's light hold and when she reached the other couple she slipped her arm through Crystal's, saying brightly, 'Rafe was just saying the sun sets in the bay. I hope we have a good view of it in the restaurant.'

They did. In fact, their table was perfect, along with everything else.

It was round about the dessert stage that Marianne realised she was thoroughly enjoying herself—unexpected in the circumstances. The four of them got on extremely well—easy talk and easy laughter—and, although she still felt there was a hint of something else hanging in the air when her glance met Rafe's, she told herself it was only her sinful imagination. He had clearly decided theirs was strictly a platonic relationship, a business friendship, nothing more. And that was good. Of course it was. Anything more would have been impossible.

Music was playing, courtesy of a small band, and couples were drifting on and off the dance floor. Andrew was looking tired and for that reason both women diplomatically said they would prefer to sit and watch the sunset rather than dance when asked. At the end of what had been a superb meal, coffee and brandy arrived, accompanied by handmade chocolates. It was after this that Rafe stood up and drew Marianne to her feet, taking her completely by surprise. Glancing at the other two, he said coolly, 'I'm going to show Marianne the view of the harbour from the terrace. We won't be long.'

Marianne's mind was racing. She was in a cleft stick here. If she refused to accompany him, it would be embarrassing for everyone, but the thought of wandering along the landscaped terraces outside the hotel in the moonlight with Rafe filled her with trepidation. But why? she asked herself in the next instant. He had been clear about how he viewed her this evening; she had nothing to fear from him.

But everything to fear from herself. She didn't try to

fight the truth. She wanted him. She had been physically attracted to men in the past—she wouldn't have accepted even a first date with someone if not—but she hadn't known what sheer animal arousal was until she had set eyes on Rafe Steed. There was something about his flagrant brand of masculinity that was all the more dangerous for its casual unconsciousness. He was what he was, he didn't have to *try*, and what he was was devastating.

'Marianne?' Rafe prompted silkily.

She became aware that Crystal and Andrew were looking at her and quickly pulled herself together. There were plenty of people outside; some folk were enjoying their coffee at the tables and chairs scattered under the stars, others were doing what Rafe had suggested and wandering along the terraces overlooking the brightly lit harbour. It wasn't as if they were going to be alone.

Once outside, Rafe took her hand and, like several times before, his height and broad-shouldered leanness made her feel fragile and feminine. They didn't speak as they strolled in the darkness scented by borders of flowers specially chosen to give out their rich perfume when night fell, but Marianne felt a trembling deep inside which no amount of silent self-disgust would refute.

'You're cold.'

To her horror she realised he'd detected her shivering and only the fact he had put it down to the cool salty breeze from the harbour prevented her from sinking through the floor. The next moment he had slipped off his jacket and put it round her slim shoulders, the scent and warmth from his body immediately encompassing her in a sensual blanket.

Her heart threatening to jump into her throat, Marianne

murmured, 'No, please have it back,' as she tried to hand the jacket to him. 'You'll be cold yourself.'

'Me? Never.' He adjusted the jacket more firmly round her shoulders. 'I'm a very warm-blooded animal,' he said, straight-faced.

'Lucky you,' she returned brightly, purposely ignoring the sexual innuendo. 'I can be cold on the warmest nights. I'm probably the only person in the world who carries a hot-water bottle in their luggage on holiday, just in case.'

The firm mouth curved. 'A hot-water bottle?' he murmured softly. 'There are other ways to be warm in bed.'

He had undone the top button of his shirt and loosened his bow-tie so it hung either side of his collar when he'd removed his jacket and it wasn't helping her equilibrium one bit. 'Perhaps,' she said primly. She determinedly changed the subject by adding, 'Some of the yachts in the harbour are truly amazing, aren't they? Do you like sailing or water sports?'

'I like all sorts of sports, Marianne.' He pulled her to a standstill, slipping an arm round her waist as they stood together looking down into the bay.

She knew the casual flirting was just part of the evening and normally such banter on a date was fun, but this wasn't a date in that sense and for the life of her she didn't know how to respond to him. Then, still gazing over the water and his voice now quiet and without amusement, he said, 'A few days ago you asked me if I loved my wife when I married her. The truthful answer to that would be that I loved the person I thought she was, but in reality she couldn't have been more different. From the moment we met she projected an image she thought I wanted and it worked. It worked very well. She reeled me in and I never suspected a thing.'

Marianne barely breathed. She sensed from the way he was speaking that he rarely talked like this, if ever.

'By the time I found out that Fiona didn't confine her sexual activities to our bed alone, probably every damn person in a fifty-mile radius except me knew. It was an…informative experience.'

Her voice barely audible, she whispered, 'I'm sorry.'

'It was a long time ago, Marianne. It taught me plenty, so in one way I should be grateful. I paid my way out of my mistake and there were no threads like kids to complicate matters. I swore then I would never marry again.'

She turned to face him for the first time. 'Why are you telling me all this, Rafe?'

'I don't know,' he said, with such boyish bemusement it wrenched at her heartstrings. 'I just want to…' he paused, shaking his head '…make it plain how I feel, I guess. Commitment, forever, family, it isn't for me. I've tried it once and once was enough. Oh, I don't mean I'm not monogamous when I'm seeing someone, that's something entirely different. I give and expect absolute fidelity. But when it's time to move on I like to think friendship replaces intimacy with no hard feelings on both sides.'

Although he had turned to face her, his features were in shadow because the lights were behind him. Was he propositioning her? Marianne asked herself dazedly. Was that it? Laying out his rules so she knew exactly where she would stand if she started a relationship with him? Which was nowhere, apparently. Quelling the rising anger, she said coolly, 'And there are women who accept those terms?

Who like what is little more than an emotionless lay?' It was crude but, in the circumstances, she felt justified.

He stiffened. 'A healthy friendship and respect for each other's independence between two members of the opposite sex is hardly that.'

'But—and correct me if I'm wrong here—the healthy friendship and respect scenario always includes sex?' Marianne asked, unable to prevent the tartness from sounding in her voice.

He stared at her, steely-eyed. 'You are deliberately mis-understanding what I'm saying.'

'On the contrary, Rafe. I think I understand you very well. We agreed a few days ago we are attracted to each other in a physical sense. This is the next step. Right?'

'No, of course not.' He watched her face as disbelief battled with anger, and he could have kicked himself. What the hell was he doing?

Everything he'd promised himself he wouldn't.

'Good, because let me make one thing perfectly clear,' Marianne said, ice in her crisp tone. 'I have absolutely no intention of sleeping with you now or at any time in the future. There may well be plenty of women out there who are grateful for the privilege of having you in their bed, but I'm not one of them. OK? No one can guarantee anything when they start dating someone, I know that, but to enter a relationship with no expectations of commitment or pos-sibility that it might be serious doesn't fit in with who I am. Just so you know.'

'Fine.' How to kill something stone dead in one easy lesson, he told himself bitterly. He looked at her standing so tensely in front of him, her small chin tilted in a way he was coming to recognise meant indomitability, and for a moment the temptation to backtrack, to refuse everything he had just said was strong. It was enough for him to sense the sticky coils of heart involvement closing round him and it frightened him to death. His voice cold, he said, 'I'm glad we've cleared the air and know where we stand. Shall we get back to the others if you're cold?'

Whipping the jacket from her shoulders, Marianne handed it to him and turned on her heel. She had only gone a yard or two when he caught at her arm, swinging her to face him. 'I'm sorry, OK?' he said, his voice gentler. 'Look, for what it's worth, I know you're the sort of woman who wouldn't be satisfied with a short affair, or even a long one, come to that. But the women I date—it suits them, Marianne. It's a two-way thing, believe me. I told you how I feel because I wanted to make it clear. That's all.'

'Well, you have.'

He could see she wasn't going to be mollified and in truth he couldn't blame her. Even a lad still wet behind the ears would have made a better job of this evening than him. The trouble was, she was like a drug and he couldn't get enough of her. He had never wanted a woman so badly without bedding her. Correction. He had never wanted a woman so badly full stop, he told himself grimly, and he was sick of cold showers at three and four in the morning. The best thing he could do was to get his butt back to the States and put an ocean between them. He knew of more than one woman who would appreciate his candour about his intentions, even if he wasn't a man who made promises.

'I shall be leaving the day after tomorrow. Is there any chance I can leave knowing we're still friends or have I blown it?' he asked, deliberately adopting a meekness he hoped would defuse the situation.

He saw the deep brown eyes weigh him up. 'You can't charm your way out of this,' she said reprovingly.

Detecting a slight softening in her manner, he took a chance and kissed her lightly on her delectable nose. She would never know the control it took when every nerve and sinew was aching to feel her body against his and her mouth open beneath his lips. 'Business all the way from here. How does that sound? And don't forget there are two other people in this equation. Crystal and my father would find it uncomfortable if we're at each other's throats, don't you think?' he asked with unrepentant persuasion.

'Believe me, you wouldn't want to know exactly what I'm thinking right now.'

He did not allow himself to question why it was so important this woman remained in his life, even if it was on the perimeter. Ruthlessly he called upon the charm she had mentioned and which had rarely let him down in the past. 'Harmony for Seacrest's sake, then? How about that?'

She stared at him a little longer and then nodded once.

CHAPTER NINE

THE next few weeks were hectic and messy with umpteen minor panics as the builders moved in but, although she only averaged four or five hours' sleep a night, Marianne welcomed the frantic pace. The knowledge that she was responsible to oversee the alterations to Seacrest virtually on her own was heavy at times, but it did mean her mind was fully concentrated on the job in hand. During the day, that was. Her dreams—which regularly featured a tall dark man with riveting blue eyes—she could do nothing about.

Andrew seemed surprisingly content to leave everything to her and Marianne had not expected this. Apart from the odd hour or two once or twice a week when he visited Seacrest with Crystal in tow, she only saw the pair of them when she called in Andrew's house for her evening meal. Although Marianne had been determined to make no regular arrangement, this had gone by the board in the first week. After chatting with Andrew one evening shortly after Rafe had left, she had come to understand he had been confined to bed after a car accident for some months before the onset of his present illness. Consequently, when the leukaemia had reared its ugly head just as he had had some hope of becoming mobile again it had struck him doubly hard. It had also meant his limbs were weak and his mental attitude low. He had apparently refused to consider any therapy, which explained a lot to Marianne.

After some diplomatic persuasion, it had been agreed she would work with Rafe's father for an hour before dinner each night, showing him how to encourage his joints to become flexible and mobile, improve his circulation and generally regain his independence. After gaining his trust, they'd gone on in leaps and bounds. She had worked out a plan of controlled activity for him during the day which Crystal oversaw, and then in the evening she completed the programme. From the beginning she had realised that Andrew's psychological battle was greater than his physical limitations, but as the weeks had flown by he had made startling progress. She knew from experience that no two patients reacted to illness or disability in the same way, and with Rafe's father the emphasis had to be always that he was in control. Once she had convinced him she did not see him as an invalid he had been putty in her hands.

Marianne had found—somewhat to her consternation—that the more she got to know Andrew, the more she liked him. For all his shouting and blustering he was a gentle man, and kind.

At the beginning of the fifth week, and two days before Rafe was due to return to England, the two of them finally had the talk Marianne had been both dreading and wishing for. After an hour's therapy they were seated at the dining-room table waiting for Crystal to serve the soup when Andrew said, 'Your parents would be proud of the way you're coping, Annie. You know that, don't you?' He had taken to calling her Annie naturally, probably because Crystal did so.

'Thank you.'

'But then they were both strong people so I'm not surprised.'

She could hear Crystal in the kitchen and, knowing she would be bringing the soup tureen any moment, Marianne gathered her courage. 'I know my mother was seeing you before she met my father,' she said in a rush before she lost her nerve. 'Rafe told me and I asked Crystal about it. They…well, they gave different versions about it and I wanted to know…' Her voice petered out. Whenever she had rehearsed this moment it had been without Andrew's calm steady gaze on her face.

'You want to know how it really was,' Andrew finished for her.

Marianne flushed. 'My mother was a good person.'

'Yes, she was, m'dear.'

'But Rafe seems to think differently.'

'Can I be frank with you?' Andrew leant forward, his lined handsome face under its shock of white hair tender. 'My son suffered quite a knock when he found out his wife was not what she seemed. He was idealistic in those days, even romantic. Nevertheless, he dusted himself off and got on with life on his own terms. I regret very much mentioning your mother to him because he misunderstood how things were. He loved his mother greatly, and for quite a while he felt I had slighted her in some way. This was not the case. I did care for your mother as a youth, Annie, but I loved my wife when I was a man. Your mother will always be a sweet memory, my first love. But Rafe's mother was my life partner, the woman who had my name and my son. When I tried to explain this to Rafe he was not in the mood to listen. Because of his experience with Fiona he had become more cynical than I had imagined.'

'So you didn't feel she chose my father because he was wealthy and you weren't?' she asked baldly, needing to bring it out into the open. 'Because of what he would give her materially?'

'Your mother was one of the most unworldly people I've ever met. I can't say I wasn't bitterly disappointed and upset at the time but I never imagined money had anything to do with her decision. She simply fell in love. Unfortunately, we can't always choose where we love. It happens like a spear sometimes, straight into the heart. Looking back, I know I knew how things were the moment I introduced them. It was as sudden as that for them both. Their faces gave them away.'

Marianne nodded, a great weight lifting. She had never doubted her mother for an instant but she had hated to think that Andrew had harboured a grudge against her parents all these years. 'Rafe hates her,' she murmured painfully.

'No. He only thinks he does.'

'That sounds very wise but isn't it the same thing?'

Andrew gave a little grunt of amusement. 'Now that could have been Gerald talking. No, I don't think it's the same thing at all. Would you like me to speak to him?'

She considered this for a moment. 'No.' Her chin lifted. 'I don't think it would make any difference, not with Rafe. He has to come to his own decision about things.'

Andrew's eyes narrowed. 'Very perceptive of you.'

Crystal chose that moment to make an appearance and

Marianne wasn't sorry. She had the feeling that Andrew was pretty perceptive, too, and the last thing she wanted was to betray herself. It disturbed her more than she would admit that Rafe forced himself into her mind the minute her subconscious took over but every night it was the same, and the eroticism of her dreams were something else. Suddenly she didn't recognise herself any more. She knew Rafe associated love with weakness and loss. He had made that abundantly plain. So why did the thought of seeing him again in the flesh cause her heart to slam like a sledgehammer?

Each night his lips met hers, each night he kissed her deeply and without reserve, leading her into an intimate place where she could taste him, feel his warmth and scent, the hard thrust of his body. And then, just when she felt she would explode from the force of pleasure welling inside her, she would wake up—alone. And sleep would be a million miles away with sexual frustration gnawing at her. Down she would pad to the kitchen, but the hot sweet milk and packet of chocolate digestives couldn't completely dispel the lingering enchantment of that phantom lovemaking. She was going to be as round as she was tall if she didn't get herself sorted.

They had all begun on their soup when the sound of a key in the lock of the front door caused them to pause. The next moment measured footsteps crossed the hall and then Rafe appeared in the doorway, tall and bronzed and smiling quietly. 'This looks very cosy,' he said evenly. 'Room for one more at the table?'

'Of course.' Crystal jumped up and for a few moments all was bustle and questions and answers as to why he was two days early.

'The Texas problem was sorted quicker than I'd envisaged,' Rafe said shortly to his father, before turning to Marianne, who had had time to compose herself after the shock of seeing him so unexpectedly. 'I hear you've been working with Dad in your role of therapist? That's kind of you, Marianne. I appreciate it.'

His gaze caught hers and she couldn't look away. The piercing blue eyes she had seen so often in her dreams were studying her face, assessing her motives. She could feel it. She nodded. 'He's doing fine.'

'Of course I am,' Andrew put in. 'I'm as strong as a horse. I've been telling you that for months, Rafe.'

'So you have.'

Marianne felt enormous relief when the sapphire gaze was directed at the older man. She knew Rafe was an expert at searching people's faces to discover their emotions because Andrew had told her so. It was one of Rafe's greatest strengths in business, his father had said proudly, and worth its weight in gold. She didn't share Andrew's enthusiasm.

The meal continued amid conversation about the business in America and how the alterations to Seacrest were progressing. To an outsider everyone would have appeared relaxed and insouciant but that couldn't have been more at odds with the way Marianne felt inside. She had expected to have time to get herself primed for Rafe's return, to bring to the fore the armour she knew it was vital to have in place with this man. And here she was in the same grubby clothes she'd been wearing all day when she had been clearing the old kitchen ready for the builders to begin knocking it about the next day, as well as keeping an eye on the work in progress, which involved walking through clouds of dust and debris. Normally she bathed and changed before coming to Andrew's, but lack of time had meant that wasn't possible today, not if she was going to fit in Andrew's hour of therapy.

It hadn't helped that her little car had refused to start and she had had to gallop the couple of miles to the village. Whenever she did walk to the cottage—and that was more often than not—she usually enjoyed the peaceful walk through high-hedged lanes, but tonight she'd arrived feeling hot and sticky.

Once the meal was finished she helped Crystal carry the dishes through to the kitchen and load the dishwasher, before popping her head round the dining-room door where the two men were sitting enjoying a brandy with their coffee. 'I'm off,' she said brightly, letting her gaze wash over both faces. 'See you tomorrow.'

'I'll walk back with you.' Rafe stood up as he spoke.

'No, you must be tired.' Even as she voiced the words she knew he wouldn't take any notice. One thing she had learnt about Rafe in the last few months was that he always did exactly what he determined to do.

'Not at all,' he said smoothly, right on cue. 'An evening walk in the fresh air is just what I need after all that travelling. I'm tired of sitting.'

As they stepped out of the front door the scents and sounds of a late summer evening surrounded them. Rafe took her arm in the familiar gesture she remembered, tucking it through his as they walked out of the drive and into the village street. 'Did Dad tell you I'd been trying to persuade him to have some therapy on his legs for months after the accident?' he asked softly. When she shook her head, he continued, 'But he dug his heels in and said he'd do it his way. By the time he realised he was making no progress the leukaemia was diagnosed.'

'He can be stubborn.' Like father, like son.

'Anyway, you're a miracle-worker and I'm grateful,' the deep masculine voice murmured before becoming silent.

Her hair was loose and a warm, salt-scented breeze caused one or two strands to drift across her cheeks as they left the village behind and continued along a lane which climbed away from the sea. The violet shadows of dusk were beginning to creep across the road as they walked, still in silence, and several times Marianne had to swallow against the tightness in her throat.

It was when they branched off into the narrower lane which bordered the cliffs and led to Seacrest that Rafe spoke again. 'How have you been?'

'Me? Busy,' she said lightly. 'How about you?'

'The same.' He paused. 'Marianne, you aren't afraid of me, are you?' There was a strange quality to his voice and she couldn't quite define it.

'Of course I'm not.' It wasn't the truth. Physically, she knew he would do nothing to hurt her. Emotionally...

'Good.' He sniffed the air appreciatively. 'I'd forgotten how good it smells here. I don't think I've ever smelt this mixture of sea and flowers and fields in the same way anywhere else. I thought my father was crazy to come back but I'm beginning to see why his birthplace could exert a pull.'

They had reached a bend in the lane where the hedgerow was low enough to see over the top of it. Below the field to their left, which sloped dramatically down to the cliffs, a panoramic view of sea and sky could be seen, the water glittering in the dying sun. 'It's the most beautiful place in the world,' she said throatily, the lovely night and the fact that Rafe was here at the side of her causing a weakness she could well have done without.

'You're beautiful.' She tensed as his hands gently pulled her to face him, enclosing her in the circle of his arms. 'I haven't been able to get you out of my head while I've been away.'

She forced a casualness she didn't feel. 'With all those gorgeous American women on hand? I can't believe that.'

'Neither could I, to be truthful, but it's a fact.' He was deadly serious now. His eyes darkened as he added, 'I took someone out to dinner when I'd been back a few days but halfway through the evening I realised I was using her as a substitute for you. It wasn't my finest moment.'

She didn't know what to say. 'I'm sorry,' she managed after a moment or two.

'You've bewitched me, do you know that?' His voice emerged husky and his eyes were a deeper blue than usual.

'Rafe—'

'I know, I know. We're different people and we want different things, but right at this moment all I want is you. Tell me you don't feel it, this primal attraction between us. Tell me your blood isn't sizzling right now.'

She made a small, ineffectual effort to shake her head but he pulled her closer against his hard body. 'We're two free agents, Marianne. There's no reason on earth why we shouldn't enjoy each other's company.'

She opened her mouth to tell him there were a hundred

reasons but his head lowered and his lips traced the outline of her mouth. 'I keep remembering the times I've kissed you,' he said against the softness of her flesh. 'And every time I get as hard as a rock and want more—much more.' He nipped at her lower lip, tasting the sweetness that was her. 'Damn it, I haven't been able to sleep, to think. For the first time in my life I've taken short cuts in an effort to get back over here to see you. What have you done to me, woman?'

He placed a hand on the small of her back to steady her as she swayed against him, using the other to lightly cup her breast.

'Rafe.' The word was a breathless whisper and she knew it wasn't the way to deal with a man like Rafe. She had to be strong, cool; she had to show him she didn't want this. But she did—so much. Desire was racing through her bloodstream, igniting nerve-endings. His hand began to move on her breast in a slow languorous rhythm that sent tremors coursing through her body and the assault on her mouth deepened, his lips and tongue creating an unbearable need.

She was vitally aware of the power in the male frame, the warmth of his body, the clean scent of his aftershave as the deliberate eroticism continued, and at the same time Marianne could feel his heart pounding like a sledge-hammer against the solid wall of his chest. He was hugely aroused and there arose in her a primitive exultation that she could cause such desire.

It was the sound of an approaching car that caused him to release her and step back a pace a few moments before the vehicle came round the bend in the road. They stood staring at each other, both breathing hard and his body trembling almost as much as hers. 'You see,' he said in a ragged voice. 'You see how it is? We only have to touch each other for fireworks to go off. Think how it would be if—'

'Stop it.' The heat was still suffusing her body but with space between them sanity had returned. 'I don't want this.'

'I don't believe you. You want me every bit as much as I want you—your body's told me so. It's too late to deny it, Marianne.'

'I'm not denying sex between us would be good,' she said shakily, 'but I want more than that. I'm not like you, Rafe. It has to mean much more than what you have told me you could give. And one day I want to get married, have a family, babies.'

'But don't you see, you could do that? I wouldn't stop you. Just because we spend time together doesn't negate you meeting someone in the future who wants the same things as you. But this is *now*. Now, Marianne, and it seems crazy we want each other so much and yet you're denying us. It doesn't make sense.'

It made perfect sense. As she stared at him everything was so clear. She had been battling to keep the knowledge that she loved him out of her consciousness for weeks but now it was almost a relief to admit it to herself. Embarking on an affair with Rafe would be emotional suicide; it was as simple as that. You didn't recover from the aftermath when a man like Rafe left—as he inevitably would—you just learnt to live with the fallout. And she wasn't prepared to do that. She valued herself more highly than that. Some women could take his terms and make them work. She couldn't. Weeks and months—maybe a year or two if she was lucky—of being near to him, part of his life, sleeping in his bed and he in hers, would be impossible to let go of.

So where would that leave her when the time came? Destroyed, that was where.

'Rafe, I can't be what you want me to be,' she said slowly, her voice still shaky but a thread of strength winding through it.

'You *are* what I want you to be.' He reached out his hand, touching the silken curtain of her hair. 'You're perfect.'

She smiled sadly. He didn't see it. In fact, he was so far from seeing it he was light years away. There had to be more to a relationship than enjoying each other physically and love needed to be a two-way thing, at least for her. Not that he knew she loved him. And he never would. 'I'm far from perfect.' Her voice was firmer. 'But I do know my own mind, Rafe. I don't want the sort of deal you're offering. OK?'

Dark colour flared across the hard cheekbones, his blue eyes narrowing. 'This is not business we're discussing, it's us. You and me.'

She nodded slowly. 'I know that. But you have carefully laid out the criteria and drawn up the contract so I couldn't possibly be under any illusion about how you see this merger progressing. Well, haven't you?' she persisted when he said nothing but continued to stare at her, his eyes narrowing still more and becoming blue slits. 'And I'm grateful, in a way. You have been nothing if not honest, and honesty is becoming a rare commodity in business these days.'

'For crying out loud,' he grated, 'this has nothing to do with business, how many times do I have to tell you? This—you and me—is something separate from Seacrest and the hotel venture.'

'Barely.' She brushed a wisp of hair from her face as the

sea breeze teased it. 'Because all your life *is* is business these days, Rafe. Your work, your love life—they are so entwined as to become one. You employ the same set of rules in one area as you do in the other. Cards on the table, logical reasons for continuing, no emotion allowed to distort the picture. It's all cut and dried. You remain in control, autonomous.'

'You're talking sheer garbage.'

'Why? Because I'm not prepared to agree to your cold-blooded proposal?' She shook her head. 'Look, I want to go home now and I'd rather continue by myself. I don't belong in your world, Rafe. I never have. And I don't want to. I might meet someone in the future who lets me down. I might get my heart broken. I might even have a marriage that fails. But I'll have tried, I'll have lived and felt rather than keeping my emotions in cold storage through fear.'

'Fear?' Now she had really caught him on the raw. 'You are saying I'm motivated by fear just because I choose to live my life without wanting the complications that come with the marriage mill? Hell, marriage is an unnatural enough state at the best of times and heavily weighted on the side of the female of the species. Love, if it even exists in the way you seem to expect, never lasts and even while it does is dependent on one person subjugating themselves to make it work. It's unhealthy at best and disastrous at worst.' He stopped abruptly.

She stared at him, knowing he had revealed far more than he had intended and that he would blame her for it. 'Like I said,' she said softly, praying she could hold back the tears until she was on her own, 'we're very different people who want different things. I don't want to fall out with you but I can't pretend to be anything other than what I am. Neither can you. We need to put an end to this, Rafe, once and for all, and move on. You do see that, don't you?'

Her knees were trembling and, more because she didn't want to sink to the ground at his feet than anything else, she forced herself to turn and begin walking away. She expected him to follow her. He didn't.

By the time she reached Seacrest her tears were blinding her. The twilight was thick now, a crescent moon high in the midnight-blue sky and the soft whisper of the Cornish sea carrying on the breeze. She didn't go into the house, making her way into the garden instead and walking down to her mother's bench where Rafe had comforted her all those weeks ago.

She didn't want to love him. She shut her eyes tight, rocking forwards and backwards with her hands clasped round her middle. She wanted to go back in time to before she had met him, before her parents had died, when she had been *happy*. She wanted to believe all those people who said love couldn't happen suddenly and what she was feeling was just animal attraction which would die in time. She wanted to, but she couldn't. She had been waiting for Rafe all her life and if she didn't marry him, she would marry no one.

She lifted her face, staring mistily into the shadows. She had done the only thing she could but it wasn't much comfort.

CHAPTER TEN

RAFE watched her go, knowing he was going to let her walk out of his life. He continued to stand frozen for a full five minutes before starting to walk, and then it wasn't back to the village, nor to Seacrest, but across the fields to the cliff path. It took a while to find a spot where he could climb down to the beach but, once there, he started to pace the sand, his mind in turmoil.

He marched up and down for an eternity before sitting on a rock which still held the warmth of the day. She was right. They were too different in their thinking for a relationship to work even for a short while. He frowned, and then looked up at the sky. It was a fine night and thousands of stars twinkled above him, the sea calm and serene as it allowed small waves to lap towards the shore. Nature had conspired to produce a backdrop of great beauty but then it often did; it was man who tended to mess the planet up, he thought darkly.

He lowered his head into his hands and listened to the sound of the sea. He sat for a long, long time.

He was a mess. He couldn't shut out the truth any longer. *He had been blocking out all manner of things for years.*

For a moment he was tempted to rise to his feet and walk back to the village, to drink brandy with his father and discuss the business, anything to evade the thoughts gathering steam in his head. Yet he had to face what his real feelings were.

When he raised his head and stared blindly into the darkness, he knew he loved her. And she was right about the fear because it scared him to death. Since the break-up with Fiona he had emerged as a respected businessman, a force to be reckoned with. He had furthered his father's business far beyond what it had been when he had first come on board, working all hours, building a small dynasty which had brought its own rewards and problems. But he had been in control. Always. And this—this was something different.

Was he too scared to make a commitment? He nodded his answer. And yet he loved her.

The other part of his brain that seemed to be having a conversation in his head came in loud and strong. He had loved Fiona, hadn't he? Had worshipped her, even. And she had led him one hell of a dance, had publicly humiliated him.

But Marianne wasn't like that.

How did he know that? Who really ever knew another person, deep inside? You heard of couples who had been together twenty, thirty years separating, one partner going off with someone new. He raked back his hair with an irritability that mirrored his father's. So it was far better never to get involved in happy-ever-after in the first place, surely?

And live your life alone?

Yes, he could do that. He nodded to the thought. That didn't scare him. He'd done it since the divorce and managed fine. Until he'd met Marianne.

So you walk away. You get on with your life and you leave her to get on with hers. In a world of men. And what happens when you hear she's with someone? What then?

He ground his teeth. He'd want to kill the guy, that was what. He swore softly.

Marianne had confronted him with the fact that he wanted to have his cake and eat it; that was it in a nutshell. She wasn't like the women he had dated the last few years and he had known that, but he had still hoped he could use the sexual attraction between them to persuade her to fall in line with what he wanted. *What sort of man was he?*

He groaned, rising abruptly and beginning to pace again. And what sort of man did she think he was? All this damn self-counselling and there was a good chance she'd laugh in his face if he did get up the courage to meet her on her terms. And he didn't want to be vulnerable again.

His insides twisting with the intensity of his emotions, he kicked at the sand savagely. Was she like her mother? Promising one thing to one man and then calmly disappearing into the bright blue yonder with another? History had a habit of repeating itself. And his father had tried to excuse Marianne's mother of any responsibility for their break-up when he'd told him what had transpired; that had been what had really got to him. All those years and he obviously still carried a torch for the woman.

And then he stopped suddenly, lifting his face to the starlit sky. Or could it be, maybe—just maybe—that the young Diane had been as devastated as his father had said she was when she had ended their relationship? His father had been adamant that the finish of their love affair had been nothing to do with Marianne's father's position in the community and the wealth that went with it. But he hadn't believed him. He hadn't wanted to. Raw and hurting as he had felt for his mother, he had needed to blame someone. He had held up his parents in his mind as the perfect couple and he hadn't liked it when he had discovered his mother had not been his father's first love. Childish, maybe. Unfair, certainly.

Feeling that he didn't know which end of him was up, Rafe continued to face his gremlins. His mobile phone rang and he answered it. It was his father, wondering where he was. He explained he had walked Marianne home—stretching the truth slightly—and then come down to the beach to clear his head of all the stress of the last weeks. His father took this at face value, or at least he didn't question his explanation, which was enough tonight.

The night was chillier but he didn't feel the cold. At some point well after midnight he began to understand. Some time during the last few months since he had met Marianne he had begun to work things out in his mind. He hadn't been aware of it but it had been happening. Which was why the couple of dates he had had with Victoria had been an effort on his part, and likewise the lady in America. He didn't know where he was going but a change had started to happen. He wasn't satisfied with his life any longer.

His brow wrinkled as he tried to catch thoughts which still didn't make sense, but after another hour or so he stood up and began to retrace his footsteps, having come to a decision. He was going to stick around here for a time, using Seacrest as the excuse. He would phone Andy Jackson tomorrow, his second in command in the States, and tell him he was in charge for the next few weeks.

When he reached the sleeping village he stood for a

moment wondering if he was absolutely sure what he was doing. There was no guarantee Marianne would want him even if he conquered his demons, and he didn't intend to broach the subject of them with her again until he was sure he could offer her what she wanted. And he was far from sure right now. All he *was* sure of was that he wanted her, needed her, loved her and the thought of another man's hands on her was unthinkable. But that wasn't enough. It had to be all or nothing. For him as well as her.

After the sort of night Marianne wouldn't wish on her worst enemy she finally gave up the fight for sleep at five o'clock and padded down to the kitchen. After making herself her first coffee of the day, she took it outside and stood and watched the sun rise, thinking of Rafe. It was a beautiful morning.

Part of her was sad that this would be the last time she would stand at the kitchen door on a summer's morning with a coffee and watch the birds squabble at the bird table beyond the flower border. Once the builders arrived they had orders to reduce the room to an empty shell ready for its makeover as a family-cum-children's area, a place where parents with energetic youngsters could come and let the children play without disturbing other guests in the drawing room. The new kitchen, on the other side of the house, was well underway but until it was finished she had arranged to have a small fridge and kettle in her bedroom, along with a tiny microwave. It would be a few weeks yet before the builders started on the extension which would be her and Crystal's accommodation.

As the birds began to sing and sunshine flooded the

garden she went inside to shower and get dressed, trying to concentrate on anything but Rafe. There was no reason to think about him any more, she told herself fiercely. OK, so she'd have to liaise with him up to a point over the next few months until Seacrest was up and running as a business, but there would be Crystal and Andrew around, too, and she would make sure everything was kept on a strict working basis. She could do this. She had no choice. One day at a time. That was what her father had always said when life had got difficult.

She heard the foreman's car scrunch onto the drive about seven o'clock. He was somewhat early but it did not matter; she was more than ready to start the day. He usually came a little while before his men and talked through the day's programme with her.

Stitching a smile onto her face, she opened the front door. The smile froze and so did she when she saw who had just unfolded himself from the front seat of what must be a hire car.

'Good morning, Marianne,' Rafe said calmly. 'Crystal said work usually commences around seven-thirty so I thought you might be up.'

She stared at him. He was freshly shaven and the light blue shirt he was wearing was tucked into the flat waistband of his casual trousers. He looked cool and perfectly at ease, and for a moment the resentment was white-hot. She'd had a sleepless night and felt like a wet rag this morning, but there was Rafe, as controlled as ever.

'Good morning,' she said stiffly.

'I thought it might be opportune to have a word with the men before they start work.' He walked towards her, unsmiling. 'And I'd like to see progress thus far if that's all right by you?'

'Of course.' She tried to match his detached, even tone but it was hard. 'It's your money that's funding this.' That sounded a little curt and by way of recompense she added, 'Would you like a coffee?'

'I'd love one.'

She turned on the doorstep and he followed her into the kitchen, glancing around as he said, 'They start work in here today, don't they?'

'Yes. Once they arrive I'll take the kettle and coffee and tea things out of the way. All the cupboards are cleared, of course. Everything's ready.'

'I didn't doubt it would be.' He perched himself on an empty worktop. 'I'll have my coffee black.'

Marianne busied herself filling the kettle and placing two of the six mugs she had kept handy for the builders on a tray, keeping her back to him as she did so. She couldn't blame him for coming to check on his investment and she had half expected he might call over the next day or two while he was in England; she just hadn't bargained for a dawn visit! And she found his presence acutely disturbing, especially after the home truths which had been exchanged the evening before. Still, she would have had to face him at some point, she told herself bracingly, so it might as well be earlier rather than later.

This comforting thought disappeared when he said in quite a different tone, 'Sleep well?'

Steeling herself to turn and face him, she brought all her will-power to bear in a polite smile. 'Not too bad. And you?'

He shrugged. 'Not a wink.'

'Oh.' She didn't know what to say, not so much because of the admission he had made but the look on his face. Gone was the cool businessman of a minute ago and in his place was the Rafe of last night. She turned round on the pretence of making the coffee and caught sight of herself in one of the glass doors of the empty cupboards. If she could see the tension lines radiating from her mouth then so could Rafe.

'We need to talk.'

She didn't reply to this, tipping hot water onto the coffee and stirring it before she nerved herself to face him again. 'It's instant, I'm afraid.'

'Did you hear what I said?'

'Rafe, we talked last night.'

'Yes, we did,' he said steadily. 'It was the first time I have really talked to a woman in years, since the break-up of my marriage, in fact. It was a painful experience.'

'I'm sorry—'

He cut her off by seamlessly continuing, 'But necessary. I see that now. Certain wounds were cauterised. Years too late perhaps, but cauterised nonetheless. Other issues were brought up to the surface, however, and they were harder to deal with. Hence the sleepless night.'

Marianne took a big gulp of her coffee. She didn't know where this was going but she needed the caffeine to cope without a doubt. She noticed her hand was shaking and hoped he hadn't. She also wished she wasn't in her oldest jeans and paint-stained top with not a scrap of make-up and her hair pulled back in a ponytail. A confidence booster, it wasn't.

'When we parted last night I spent some hours on the beach.' He took a pull of his own coffee, his eyes narrowing over the steam rising from the mug. 'By the time I went back to the house I'd decided to stay in England for a few weeks, but I still wasn't sure what I wanted. No, that's wrong. I wasn't sure what I could offer.'

'Offer?' She stared at him, her eyes huge in the paleness of her face. She wished she hadn't taken the breakfast stools out of the way the day before when she had cleared the room. She would have given anything to sit down and control the trembling in her legs.

He nodded. 'But then, as I sat up all night, things became clear.'

Marianne studied his handsome face, taking in the blue, blue eyes, the chiselled facial structure, the firm mouth. He was so composed, she thought weakly. So in control. Nothing really touched him.

And then he disabused her of this idea when he uncoiled himself from the breakfast bar and stood up, setting his mug down. His expression remained impassive but she saw something in his eyes that caused her heart to race. 'Can I ask you something before I continue?' he said softly.

She nodded, trying to still the rapid beating of her heart.

'You've said often enough we're very different people and I accept that. You've also said you acknowledge that physically we would be good together. But—'

'What?'

'Could you see yourself wanting to get to know me? As a person, not—' He paused. 'Not as someone who gives you the privilege of their company in bed.'

The words she had thrown at him were without heat but she knew they had cut deep. Emotion surged through her so rawly she lowered her eyes. She couldn't let him see how he affected her. 'I'm not sure what it is you're saying,' she prevaricated.

He waited until she raised her gaze to his before he said, 'It's simple.'

'No, nothing's simple with you,' she responded before she considered her words. 'You've told me you are completely satisfied with your life the way it is. That you like to be free, without commitment of any kind. That you would never dream of getting emotionally involved with a woman again. That's what you've *told* me.'

'I lied. Not consciously, but the man I've become is not the man I want to continue to be. Does that make sense?'

'Last night you were so sure, Rafe.'

'I know. And I'm not expecting you to believe me in one fell swoop.'

'But how could you change so radically?'

It was the same question he had asked himself in the early hours when he had sat by his bedroom window looking out over his father's dark garden. And when the answer had come it had been that which had suddenly made everything so clear. 'You didn't answer me when I asked you if you would spend some time with me,' he urged her gently.

Marianne hesitated. Everything in her wanted to say yes but she was terrified, too. He had been so sure of what he wanted and what he didn't want. This man, if he did but know it, held her heart in the palm of his hand and she wasn't sure if he would throw it away when—if—he tired of her. She stared at him. Yesterday she would have been sure it would be a case of *when* he tired of her but something had changed. Now there was an *if* there, too. It was a faint hope but could she ignore it? Aware that she could be opening herself up for heartache on a scale she'd never known before, she said, 'Yes.'

She hadn't realised how tensely he had been holding himself until he relaxed, and then he smiled. 'Good.'

His hand was gentle under her chin as he lifted her mouth to his and immediately her lips opened at his probing. The fire which was just waiting to ignite every time they touched blazed into being and he moved his body slightly, pressing her against the worktop so he could feel every soft curve, every contour.

Her hands slid up around his neck as she returned the need to be close, their bodies a mutual aphrodisiac that was more potent than any man-made brew.

'You're beautiful, inside and out,' he murmured throatily. 'Warm, soft, intoxicating. For weeks I haven't been able to sleep properly for thoughts of you in my arms.' He moved his hands over her body and she felt her nipples tighten under his light touch, their tips straining against the thin material of her top. 'I want to eat you alive, do you know that? Devour you. Fill your body and your mind until there is only me in your world.'

She trembled; she couldn't help it. Last night she had thought things were over for good and now... A soft warmth was spreading deep within her body as his hands and mouth worked their magic. His hard muscular frame, the sexy smell of his aftershave, the words he was muttering against her skin were taking her somewhere she had never been before. She felt as though she were one aching cell and if he didn't relieve the pressure inside her she would die.

And then his mouth became slower, gentler, his hands

settling round her waist and his body no longer pressed against hers. Drugged, she lifted heavy eyes to him to see what was wrong and saw him looking at her with an odd expression on his face. 'We're not going to rush this. It's too important,' he murmured hoarsely. 'I want you to trust me—really trust me—and I have to earn that. I don't want physical desire to cloud the issue and make you do something you'll regret. Or at least be unsure about. You're not the kind of woman who can give herself without it meaning more than—' He shook his head as though he didn't know how to continue.

Marianne pulled away slightly. Rafe had told her he'd indulged in an active sex life since his divorce and this was clearly a first for him. With her body burning and her head swimming with the impassioned words he had muttered, she didn't know whether to laugh or cry. In the event she did neither. Controlling the urge to fling herself on him and ask him to take her right there, on the kitchen floor, she said, 'You're a very surprising man. Do you know that?' aiming to keep her voice from trembling. Miraculously it didn't.

She was rewarded by his smile. It was rueful and yet carried something that made her toes curl. 'Is that good?'

Before his apparent change of heart, he had been dangerous. Now her senses were telling her he was lethal. Heeding the inner voice, Marianne took her cue from Rafe. 'Possibly,' she said with a lightness she was proud of in the circumstances. 'Now, shall I show you over the house before the builders arrive and you can see how far we've got? The bedrooms which needed an *en suite* bathroom have been completed but everything, including the others, needs decorating before we recarpet and change the furnishings and fixings, of course. It makes sense to leave all the house and have it done together. The new kitchen's coming along OK but we've decided to leave the walkway and the new build for the flat for now and concentrate on this side of the house, getting this room converted and then building the extension for the two disabled suites.'

'Fine.' He drained his coffee, his eyes never leaving her face.

'Rafe.' She hesitated but she had to ask. 'Exactly how long do you plan to be around?'

His jaw flexed. 'Exactly? I'm not sure. I've got a good guy in the States who'll take care of things up to a point but it's asking for trouble to take my eye off the ball for too long. Ours may have to be a transatlantic relationship some of the time.'

Marianne nodded. That wasn't a problem. The problem was that the enormity of the step she was taking was beginning to dawn. He hadn't made any promises, any guarantees. When she had asked him what had changed his mind so fundamentally he'd evaded the issue. She believed him absolutely when he said he was rethinking his life but that still didn't mean he would fall in love with her and, even if he did, if he would want her for ever.

But she wanted to take the chance. The blue gaze was on her and she took a deep breath. 'I can do transatlantic,' she said steadily, 'as long as the time is weighted on this side of the ocean.'

'It will be.' His voice was quiet and intense. 'Believe me, it will be.'

CHAPTER ELEVEN

THE next month was the most deliriously happy of
Marianne's life, in spite of all the hard work during the day
at Seacrest. Even that was enjoyable because Rafe arrived
most mornings and stayed with her throughout the day
before he went home to change to take her out in the evening.

They didn't always go too far afield. Sometimes he
arrived with a picnic Crystal had prepared and they took the
basket down to the beach below the house where the waves
rolled gently on the clean warm sand. They would walk and
swim and explore the rock pools before eating, then stretch
out under the dying sun and relax. At twilight they often had
the beach all to themselves and that was when they began
to talk, or at least when Rafe did. Marianne found he could
express himself better when the shadows of night mellowed
the bright light of daylight hours, and the sunsets were
glorious. She heard about his childhood, which had been
very happy on the whole although he hadn't seen much of
his father, who had been building the business up and
working long hours and weekends. For that reason he had
been close to his mother and very protective, that much
Marianne came to understand and it explained a lot. He told

her the bitter truth concerning his marriage and divorce and the life he had led since, some of which she found hard to hear. Occasionally she asked questions but mostly she let him talk and slowly she built up a picture of the complicated enigma that was Rafe.

They went to antique markets most Sundays before Rafe took her out to lunch, wandering among the stalls and lingering over the odd item that caught their eye. On one excursion Rafe bought her an exquisite little pearl and silver brooch set in the shape of a small hoop, each tiny seed pearl a flower with intricately worked silver leaves around it.

It was a relaxing, idyllic time and the weather continued to hold, one hot summer's day following another. The sun tanned Marianne's skin and highlighted her hair until it was more silver-blond than golden, emphasising her dark eyes and giving her elfin loveliness a fragility that made her look far younger than her twenty-seven years. Her days and nights were so filled with Rafe it seemed impossible he hadn't always been there, his heated kisses and lovemaking introducing her to a sensual world she realised she'd had little experience of before.

But he always stopped before things went too far. Whether they were alone at Seacrest or on the beach, he never allowed himself to lose control. And she didn't know how she felt about that.

Marianne was standing in her bedroom looking out of the window into a balmy summer's night after a wonderful evening at the restaurant they had first gone to with Crystal and Andrew. The meal had been delicious but it had been the hours on the dance floor she had liked best, held close in Rafe's arms for most of the time, breathing in the smell and feel of him and noticing the envious glances from some of the other female diners.

She frowned. Some of those women had been very beautiful and she fancied more than one would have been happy to ditch the man they were with if Rafe had lifted a little finger. Which brought her back yet again to the question which had been nagging at her for the last few days. What on earth was Rafe doing with her when he only had to raise an eyebrow to get anyone? And why, if he wanted to be with her, hadn't he taken their love-making to its natural conclusion?

In her relationships before him, it had always been her who had put on the brake when things got too steamy. She had been close to going all the way several times but it had never seemed quite right; she had never imagined herself with the man in question forever. And somehow, with the example of her parents' blissful marriage in front of her, she had wanted forever when she gave herself. Most of her friends had laughed their heads off when they'd discussed their love lives and she had admitted how she felt, but it hadn't persuaded her to go against what she felt. Just the opposite, in fact. And now she had met the man who was her forever and there was certainly no question of having to fight him off, which was pretty ironic when you thought about it.

He had said they needed time to get to know each other. She bit on her bottom lip, worrying it with her teeth. But in the last month they had been together nearly every day and certainly every night. They had packed months and months into a few weeks and discussed everything under the sun. How much getting to know each other did he want? And what was lacking in her that she couldn't inflame him to a point where he lost control? Where the decision to go further would be up to her at least?

And if that happened? If he did want more? What then? Was she absolutely sure he would never leave her or was there still the possibility that one day he could walk away and leave her worse than dead, because without Rafe there would be nothing in the world to interest her, nothing to bring her happiness and joy. And he had never said he loved her. In the last weeks he had never once said that, and how could she give herself without knowing her love was returned?

She was going round in circles. She made a sound of deep irritation in her throat. Why couldn't she just take each day as it came and forget the self-analysis once she was alone?

Because she loved him too much.

She shook her head at herself. And soon she would face a goodbye of sorts because he would be returning to America for a while. Crystal had confided that Andrew was becoming increasingly concerned at how long Rafe had been away from their business, although Andrew had not mentioned this to her and neither had Rafe. Not that she saw so much of Andrew these days since Rafe had been in England. Crystal had taken over the therapy sessions after she'd told the older woman what to do and it had proved a great success. Crystal and Andrew seemed to be getting on like a house on fire whenever she visited the cottage, and Andrew was looking the best he had in years, according to Rafe. Andrew and Crystal were going to miss each other when Crystal resumed her place at Seacrest.

Oh, why was life so complicated these days? And why, *why* had she badgered Crystal to find out from Andrew what Rafe's wife had looked like? It had been from that point her insecurities had grown. Generously curved and voluptuous she definitely was not, and apparently that was the type of woman Rafe always favoured. She would have done well to heed the old adage that curiosity killed the cat or, in this case, her peace of mind.

Sleep. Marianne nodded to the thought. She needed to turn off her mind and get some sleep or else she would be fit for nothing in the morning. All the agonising in the world wouldn't change the way Rafe saw them as a couple. In the final analysis, it was up to him.

When the insistent ring of her mobile phone brought her groaning from sleep, Marianne felt as though she had only been in bed for two or three hours. Then she realised there was a good reason for that; it was only four o'clock in the morning.

Dozily she reached for the phone, which she always placed on her bedside cabinet each night since she had been sleeping alone in the house, clicking on the overhead spotlight from the switch at the side of the headboard as she mumbled, 'Yes?'

'Marianne, it's Rafe. I'm sorry to ring you at such an hour but I need to get back to the States immediately. There's been a fire in one of the hotels and people are hurt. I'm in the car outside your house on my way to the airport but I didn't want to leave without saying goodbye in person. Could you come down and let me in for a minute?'

'Yes, of course.' She was already out of bed and pulling on her robe, not bothering with slippers as she opened the bedroom door and flew downstairs.

When she flung open the front door he was standing in front of her, and her exhilaration that he hadn't wanted to go without saying goodbye was dampened by the expression on his face. Before she could say a word, he said, 'It's bad, apparently. The hotel's gutted and a family in one of the top-floor rooms got trapped. The firefighters got them out eventually but the father is in a bad way and the two kids. I don't know if it was the fire or the smoke.'

'Oh, Rafe.' Horrified, she held out her arms and he stepped forward into them. They clung together for a moment before he kissed her, a hungry kiss that sought comfort.

'I feel I should have been there,' he said wretchedly. 'The annual review of that property was one due in the last month that Andy undertook. Don't get me wrong, he's a good guy and he won't have missed anything but I always do them. Dad and I always made health and safety our top priority.'

'You can't be everywhere doing everything.'

'I know, I know. I'm not thinking straight.' He pulled her into him again, kissing her hard so the warm scent of his body surrounded her. They swayed together for a moment, neither of them able to deny their mutual need, and then his arms tightened until she was lifted onto her toes, clinging to his broad shoulders, her head thrown back as he kissed her mouth, her neck, her throat.

'I have to go.' His voice was hoarse. 'I don't want to but I have to go. I'll miss my flight.'

'Yes, yes.'

But still they didn't let go of each other, kissing with a starving intensity as though they were parting for good. As always it was Rafe who gained control first, gently putting her from him but still supporting her trembling body as he

said, 'I'll ring you and let you know how things are, OK?
But it might be hectic…'

'No, that's OK, I understand. Just ring when you can. I
hope the children are all right, the father, too.'

There was a blue flame in the piercing eyes as he gazed
down at her. 'We have to talk. You know that, don't you?
We can't go on as we are.'

She nodded. 'But for now you have to go or you'll miss
your flight. Promise me you'll drive carefully. This is the
wrong side of the road for you, don't forget.'

'I'll be fine.' He stepped back and into the night after
one last kiss. 'Go back to sleep.'

She watched him slide into the car and remained
standing in the doorway as it purred out of the drive, his
arm waving out of the window. She remained standing
there until the night air made her shiver and then she slowly
shut the door, climbing the stairs to bed, where she lay
wide-eyed until it was time to get up.

Rafe phoned her from the plane but it was a quick call and
she could tell his mind was already in America. Knowing
the sort of man he was, she had expected nothing less. She
had walked down to see Andrew and Crystal once she had
let the builders in and work was underway, and she could
tell Rafe's father was anxious, both about the plight of the
family who had been hurt and the repercussions it might
have for the business.

It was a full twenty-four hours before Rafe called again
and he had been on her mind constantly, awake and asleep.
She could tell he was tired and working on automatic; exhaustion was in every syllable he uttered, but the news

was better than it might have been. The two children were apparently out of danger, they had been suffering from smoke inhalation, but the father had been badly burnt trying to rescue them and wasn't out of the woods by any means. Investigations were proceeding as to the cause of the fire and more would be known in the next few days.

Marianne didn't prolong the call, urging him gently to get some sleep before she said goodbye, but once it was finished she paced about the house for some time, needing him, wanting him. But she had to get used to this if they were going to have any sort of relationship at all, she warned herself later that day. America was where his home was—he had a modern bachelor pad full of gimmicks and gadgets, according to Andrew—and where he worked. His whole life was there. His wider family of aunts and uncles and cousins on his mother's side, his friends, his *history*.

It wasn't a comforting thought to brood on but she could not get it out of her head. When he had been here with her, when her whole being had been swept up in the wonder of it all, she hadn't really considered the practicalities of a long-distance relationship. Now she could think of little else as problems—or potential problems—were rearing their heads. But they would work it out. They had to.

The next day Marianne was on tenterhooks waiting for the phone to ring, but when it did it was never Rafe. She went to bed angry with herself for being so disappointed. He'd told her he was going to be tied up with all manner of problems and life would be hectic, she reminded herself fiercely. It didn't mean he didn't want to speak to her, merely that he was unable to. He was dealing with such an awful situation—of course that had to come first. Those poor children, and their father and mother… It was terrible for them all.

It wasn't as if she didn't have more than enough to keep her busy here either. The new kitchen was now up and running but in need of more appliances. The old kitchen had been transformed into a lovely bright and sunny family room and she needed to choose furniture and toys for that, along with a big TV, CD player and computer. The suites for disabled guests had been completed the day before and again were now awaiting her attention regarding furnishings, colour schemes and the like.

Tomorrow would be Saturday and the builders did not come at the weekend, but on Monday morning they were due to start the walkway and construction of the flat where she and Crystal would live. She found she had mixed feelings about this. One, because it would be strange to be living in Seacrest but separate from it, too. Two, once this last section of the project was finished she would have to fulfil her part of the bargain and become a fully fledged hotelier and she didn't know how she would take to it. Certainly she would be dancing attendance on the guests and her life would not be her own in the same way it had been. Three, with her working all hours and Rafe halfway across the world, she was frightened he would begin to cool in his affections. And what if the hotel didn't succeed? What if she and Crystal failed miserably? That would put a strain on her and Rafe's relationship, too.

She went to sleep worrying and woke up worrying, and when she came in from doing some weeding in the garden she had put off for weeks she could have cried when she realised she hadn't had her mobile with her and had missed a call from Rafe. She listened to his deep smoky voice but it sounded different, somehow, coming from all those miles away. He was obviously at some meeting or restaurant or other because there was a hubbub in the background and laughter now and again.

'Hi, Marianne. It's Rafe. I'm sorry you're not able to pick up because this is the last time I'll be able to phone over the weekend. Just to let you know they've discovered the father apparently left a cigarette burning—in a non-smoking hotel.' The last had been grim but he went on, 'Obviously the poor guy paid for his mistake big time. He's going to pull through, by the way, and the kids are fine now and home with their mother. Look, the builders won't be coming back on Monday. I thought I'd better let you know. Don't worry about it though, it's all in hand.'

Marianne's brow wrinkled as she stared at her mobile. Not coming? But why hadn't they contacted her? Why Rafe, who was on the other side of the world? That didn't make sense. In fact, thinking about it, it was damn insulting.

She didn't have time to ponder further because he went on, 'Just let everything remain as it is until I'm back and then I can sort it, OK?' And then she heard it. Distinctly. A woman's throaty laugh and then a voice saying, 'Rafe? Aren't you done yet? Come on, darling. I'm absolutely starving.'

There was a muffled sound next as though he had put his hand over the phone, and then his voice came again, saying, 'I have to go but I'm hoping to be back the middle of next week. We can talk then and I'll explain—' He paused, clearly thinking better of what he had been about to say. 'We can talk then,' he said again. 'Bye, sweetheart.'

His voice had softened on the last two words, becoming

warm and silky, but he could have yelled them for all the good it did. *He was with a woman.* She stared at the phone and nearly threw the offending article at the window. He had phoned her while he was with a woman. She felt sick, her stomach churning so badly she had to sit down on the sofa. And what had he meant about the explaining bit? There had been something odd about it and she wasn't imagining it.

Her heart thudding so hard it threatened to jump out of her chest and her ears ringing, she sat for some minutes trying to compose herself. Think, think, she told herself. She could be letting her mind run away with itself here. That woman—she didn't have to be a date. She could be…her thinking process hiccuped and then went on…a business colleague or something of that sort. It was possible. It was—it *was* possible. Oh, God, please let it be, she prayed desperately. Please, please don't let him *be* with her. She wouldn't be able to bear it.

She sat in numb misery for some time, the lunch she had come in to prepare forgotten. She had to trust him. That was what you did if you loved someone. She couldn't think the worst of him. He had been so genuine that morning he had called to see her and said he wanted to give them a chance.

But what if the last weeks hadn't meant the same to him as they had to her? What if the pull of his old life was stronger? They had laughed together, walked together, visited a hundred different places and talked deeply about their lives, but never once had he said the words she had been longing to hear. That he loved her. But then she had known he was a man who did not betray his feelings easily at the best of times, and yet he had opened up to her in a way she knew he hadn't to anyone else. He wasn't that good an actor that he could have fooled her on that point.

She chewed her thumb nail down to the quick and then fixed herself a sandwich before returning to the weeding. The sky was blue, the air warm and birds were twittering happily as they sunned themselves in the trees surrounding the garden. Crazy, but she wished it was raining. She wished there was a gale force wind blowing and everything was dank and gloomy. She wouldn't feel so at odds with her surroundings then.

She continued to mull over the conversation with Rafe for the next hour, after which she came to a decision. She had the foreman's mobile number for emergencies. She would give him a ring and at least find out what was happening to prevent them keeping to the plan. That hadn't seemed right. There had definitely been something in Rafe's voice that she couldn't place.

He answered straight away and when she explained the reason for her call there was a blank silence on the other end of the phone for some moments. Just when she was about to speak, he said, 'Have you spoken to Rafe about this, love?'

'I told you, he said you weren't going to come but it was all in hand and he'd deal with it when he got back. I can't understand why you didn't ring me, George, and furthermore I think I'm entitled to an explanation. Have you got problems on another job? Is that it? I'd like to think you know I would be reasonable and—'

'Look, love, it wasn't me who rang Rafe but the other way round.'

'What?' She frowned. 'I don't understand.'

'He rang and said he wanted us to hold our horses for a few days. That's as much as I know, all right? He said he'd cover it financially when I pointed out we'd got an agreement, but he was adamant he didn't want any more work doing on the house till he'd spoken to me in person. I asked him if he was dissatisfied with our work and he said no, it wasn't anything like that. And then that was it.' He paused. 'Rum going on, if you ask me.'

Marianne agreed. It was a rum going on.

'Does the old un, his dad, know what's going on?' George said after a second or two.

'I don't know.' She hadn't wanted to bother Andrew—he was already so worried about the problem in America—but now she felt she had to. 'I'll get in touch with him.'

'You do that, love. And you might point out we've another job after yours and we can't put it back by much. He's paying us to stand round kicking our heels the way I see it, and each day we don't work is a day lost.' George had a habit of stating the obvious.

Marianne changed out of her grubby jeans and top into a light cotton dress after she had washed her hands, brushing her hair through. She decided to walk to the cottage and as she passed the spot where she and Rafe had talked that momentous night she felt a slight chill in the breeze which hadn't been there the day before. September was upon them and the summer was nearly over, she thought with a shiver which had nothing to do with the weather.

When she reached the cottage it was to find Andrew dozing in a deckchair in the garden after his lunch and Crystal busy baking in the kitchen. Rather than wake Andrew, she sat with Crystal in the kitchen, the delicious smell of homemade bread filling the room. Crystal was the only person she knew who made all her own bread and pastry.

'He's done *what*?' Crystal stopped what she was doing and stared at her in amazement when Marianne explained the reason for her visit. 'Well, I'm sure Andrew knows nothing about it or he would have said.'

'I can't understand it, Crystal. And he was…strange. It was an odd phone call altogether, to be honest. He…he had a woman there with him.'

'A woman?' Crystal's eye sharpened on Marianne's troubled face. 'Someone who works for him, you mean? A business colleague?'

Marianne shrugged. 'She called him darling.'

'Oh, Annie.' Crystal sat down very suddenly on one of the kitchen stools. 'Andrew said—' She stopped abruptly.

'What?' Marianne stared at her. 'What did Andrew say?'

'Nothing—I shouldn't have said.'

'Yes, you should.' There was a lead weight in her stomach. 'What did he say, Crystal?'

'Nothing really. I mean, he doesn't know anything—' Crystal stopped abruptly. 'What I mean is, he had reservations about you and Rafe. He was worried for you. Not that he doesn't think Rafe cares for you, that's been apparent all along, but after Fiona Rafe swore he'd never settle down again. And you, well, you're not the sort of person for a brief affair, are you? And I know you like Rafe. More than like him, perhaps?'

'Do you think he's decided to pull out of the hotel venture?' Marianne asked numbly.

'No, no, I'm sure not. Why would he do that?'

Because he felt he'd got in way over his head here?

Because withdrawing from the deal would mean he could cut his losses and run? The expenditure so far would mean nothing to him; he could take that in his stride and barely notice it. And perhaps he thought he had set her up with a nice renovated property as compensation? Certainly Andrew hadn't got as involved as Rafe had expected. Rafe's father seemed perfectly happy spending all his time with Crystal. Maybe he thought that with the hotel idea squashed, Crystal might take on the role of permanent housekeeper to his father? That would round things up nicely. Drawing on all her strength, she managed to say calmly, 'I don't know why he would pull out, Crystal. In fact, I think I don't know him at all. I thought I did…' Her voice trailed away.

'You say he said he's coming back the middle of the week?'

Marianne nodded.

'Then would you not mention it to Andrew before then, for my sake? He's been so worried about this fire in America and I don't want anything else to upset him and put him back a bit. He's done so well the last weeks and he's such a dear man—' Crystal stopped suddenly, as though aware she had said too much.

Marianne stared at Crystal. How could she have been so blind to what was happening under her nose? But she had been so obsessed with Rafe that nothing else had registered. Her voice soft, she said, 'Does Andrew feel the same, Crystal?'

Crystal's plump face turned a vivid shade of pink. Silently she nodded. 'We didn't plan for it to happen and Andrew hasn't told Rafe yet but last night he asked me to marry him. Since he's been over here he's gone into remission but there are no guarantees and we want to make the most of every moment.' She stopped. 'Oh, Annie, I didn't want to tell you like this.'

'I'm so glad for you both.' Stepping forward, she hugged Crystal hard, her head spinning. Crystal and Andrew. *Crystal and Andrew.* But why not? Why not, indeed? Thinking about it, they were perfect for each other. 'You deserve this,' she said warmly. 'No one deserves happiness more than you.'

'Stop it, you're making me cry.'

They both cried and then Crystal made a pot of coffee and they sat together, discussing when and where the nuptials could take place. 'Andrew wants to tell Rafe face to face,' Crystal said quietly a little later when Marianne got up to go. She was thrilled for Crystal and she had meant every word she said but she needed to be on her own and consider what this new complication meant. 'He thought a lot of his mother and Andrew isn't sure how he'll feel.'

'He'll be as pleased as I am,' Marianne said warmly, and she meant it. 'He likes you very much, Crystal, and he knows you've been so good for his father over the last little while. He wouldn't begrudge you both your happiness.'

'I hope so.' Crystal gave a nervous little smile. 'But Rafe's so hard to figure out, isn't he?'

Oh, yes.

She took her time walking home. Once there, she wandered round the house for a long time, stroking a piece of furniture here, touching a picture there, tears coursing down her face. Something was terribly wrong. She knew it.

Eventually she walked out into the garden, taking a book she knew she wouldn't read and making her way to the bench near the wall. Purple shadows were already stretching their long fingers over the lawn and the birds were busy having their last meal before night fell. She sat and watched a blackbird stamping on the ground to bring a worm he had spotted to the surface, his bright black eyes checking on her every so often to make sure she was staying still. He flew off after his meal, singing as he went.

She wasn't going to call Rafe. She looked back at the house, dozing gently in the late evening sunshine, sun-spangled shadows bathing its white walls. And she wouldn't pick up the call if he phoned her. The next time she spoke to him, she wanted it to be face to face. Whatever had happened, whatever had changed—and she was now positive something had—she wanted to hear it from him in person. The temptation to start questioning him if she spoke to him before he was back in England would be too strong and she didn't want to burst into tears on him. She was going to get through this with some dignity, no matter what happened. Her back straightened slightly and her jaw tightened. She would have all the time in the world to shout and scream and cry an ocean once it was over and she was alone.

Marianne's throat constricted. 'Stop it,' she said sternly. She wasn't going to be like this. Whatever happened in the next few days, when she saw Rafe again, she would cope. Anything else was not an option.

CHAPTER TWELVE

RAFE phoned three times before he left America the following Wednesday and, true to her word, Marianne did not speak to him. By the third call his voice had been flat and cool. It did not intimidate her as it would have done just days earlier. 'So you've finally realised I'm not as stupid as I look,' she said grimly to the telephone when she had listened to his message. 'Good. Because if you expect me to fall on your neck and beg you to make a go of things, you picked the wrong girl.'

Then she closed her eyes and leant back in the sofa. Her body was so tense it hurt. She had gone through every emotion known to man in the last few days but one thing remained constant. She loved him. More fool her.

Thursday dawned cold and wet, sea mist swirling in the garden when she opened her bedroom curtains and the whole world was grey. From experience, Marianne knew the weather could change in hours; by that afternoon the view could be bathed in sunlight and the air warm. She hoped it would remain as it was. It suited what was going to happen so much better.

She forced herself to eat a slice of toast although she had

never felt less like food in her life and then settled down with a pile of brochures on colour schemes. She had absolutely no idea why she was continuing to plan out each room in the house except that if she didn't do something she would go mad. One thing was for sure, if Rafe did pull the plug on the hotel idea—and she was now sure he was going to—Seacrest belonged to him. Even if he suggested she live here, she couldn't. Crystal was OK now, she didn't have to worry about her any more, so she would become a free agent. She could move back to London and find herself a job and take up her old life. She had been happy before Rafe. She would be happy again.

Oh, who was she kidding? She stared aimlessly at the scattered brochures, wishing with all her heart she could have just one hug with her mother. She would have given everything she possessed to have her parents back. She brushed a hand over her eyes. But they had gone. She was on her own and she was a grown woman. She took a deep breath and picked up the nearest brochure.

The doorbell rang just after lunch and the English weather had done one of its unique turnabouts and banished every trace of sea mist. Although the air was cooler than it had been for some time, the sun was shining when she opened the door to Rafe.

'Hello, Marianne,' he said quietly. 'Why haven't you answered my calls?'

She stared at him. He needed a shave and he looked tired. It increased his appeal about one hundred per cent.

'Can I come in?' he asked, still in the same quiet voice.

She stood aside in answer and he passed her into the hall but there he waited for her.

'Well?' he said, making no effort to touch her. 'I take it you haven't lost your phone?'

'No, I haven't lost my phone.'

'Then why the hell have you refused to talk to me?' he bit out with a suddenness that made her jump.

She recovered almost immediately. 'You said you wanted to talk to me,' she said grimly. 'So talk.'

'What?' He stared at her as though she had lost her senses.

'On the phone, you said you needed to explain something. Could it be the reason you told the builders to stop work? I phoned George,' she added when he didn't react. 'I needed to know what was happening.'

'I told you to wait until I got back. It was only a couple of days, damn it.'

'I needed to know what was happening,' she repeated tonelessly. 'You call from America and tell me work on the house has stopped—' *she was not going to mention the woman, she had promised herself that* '—and then expect me to sit here just twiddling my thumbs without any proper explanation? I don't think so.'

'What's the matter, Marianne?'

Struggling for calmness, she said, 'Funny, but that's exactly what I was going to ask.' A shaft of sunlight shone through the hall window and picked out each feature of his dark countenance. Every fibre of her being was calling out to him but doggedly she stood there, refusing to weaken. 'Would you like to tell me why you've stopped work on Seacrest?'

'Can we sit down?'

She inclined her head towards the drawing-room door in way of reply and after a moment of searching her face, his blue eyes unreadable, he turned and led the way.

Contrary to his words, however, he remained standing when he faced her. Again the piercing eyes searched her face and then he said, 'Something tells me I haven't handled this very well.'

It wasn't what she had expected but she couldn't afford to show any emotion. 'Before you left, the night you came to tell me about the fire, you said we couldn't go on as we were. Then I hear work has stopped on the house.' She drew in a steadying breath. 'You're clearly having second thoughts about—' she had been about to say *us* but changed it to '—the project.'

'Yes, I am.'

Her stomach turned and she felt sick. But she had known it so she shouldn't be surprised, she told herself silently. 'I see.'

'I'm not sure you do. Look—' he raked a hand through his hair '—I don't pretend to be the most intuitive of men. All this talk about reading body language and the hidden signals, it's beyond me. I know you want me physically, that's not in question, but I'm not sure how you see the future. I mean—*me* in the future, long-term.' He stopped abruptly. 'Hell, do you know what I mean?'

Dredging up an answer through the confusion she was feeling, she said shakily, 'Are you asking me if I see us together for a long time?'

'No, I'm asking you if you see us together for ever.' And then he was at her side, taking her in his arms as he said, 'I'm doing this all wrong. This wasn't how it was supposed to be, damn it. And I didn't want to rush you, to make you say anything you didn't want to say. But I'm not the most patient of men, my love, and I'm not sure how much I can take. I need to know— No, I need to tell you how I feel first. Then it's up to you how we proceed.'

He moved her from him slightly. 'I love you, Marianne. I never thought I would say that again but it's true. I spoke so much garbage when we first met so I have to make it absolutely clear now, I know that. I love you. I knew I loved you some time ago but I had to sort out my head and mean it when I proposed marriage and kids and the rest of it. I should have done it weeks ago but I was afraid.'

'Afraid?' she whispered, barely able to breathe through the welling emotion. 'Of what?'

'You. The power you have over me. The power to hurt. Of you saying you don't think you can love me.' He swallowed hard. 'I've had to face the fact I'm a coward where you're concerned.'

'Rafe—'

'I was a swine when we first met and we couldn't have got off to a worse start, I accept that. All the things I said about your parents, your mother, it was my own hang-ups working through. I'm not proud of it but you need to know I don't think like that any more. Dad and I had some long talks about stuff. It was painful for both of us but it cleared the air. He's got regrets about building the business at the cost of missing time—family time—when I was young, but I see now it wasn't because he didn't love my mother enough.'

'You'd been thinking that?' she murmured, her senses so taken up with the feel and closeness of him she was having difficulty concentrating. And he'd spoken of marriage, of children, hadn't he?

He nodded. 'Marianne, I can't promise you I'd be the easiest man to live with. I'd get it wrong sometimes and make a mess of things, but one thing I can promise you is that you've got my heart and soul for eternity. I love you, I'll always love you.'

'Oh, Rafe.' She didn't know she was crying until he brushed the tears from her cheeks. 'Rafe, why didn't you say? I've been thinking all sorts of things, that you wanted to finish it.'

'Us? You thought I wanted out?' he said with absolute incredulity. 'What do you think the last month has been about? I've laid myself bare. I've never talked to anyone like I've talked to you.'

'But you never said you loved me.'

'I didn't want to pressure you, not after everything that happened at first. You needed to be able to see the real me, to know if you could love the real me. Since Fiona it's all been superficial. I was playing a game, Marianne. Being what the woman in question wanted.'

So he couldn't get hurt again. A sob burst from her throat. 'I've loved you all my life,' she whispered. 'Before I knew you I loved you and I could never stop now I've met you, whatever happened.'

He bent his head and brushed his mouth slowly over hers. 'Will you marry me?' he murmured thickly. 'Will you be my wife and the mother of my children?'

Her grip on him tightened and she gazed up into the blue eyes that held her heart. 'Yes,' she said. And when he kissed her again the world stopped spinning.

It was much later, when they had loved and talked and loved some more, that Marianne led him through to the kitchen to fix him something to eat, after he admitted he hadn't had a meal for the last twenty-four hours. 'I just wanted to get home to you,' he said softly, 'and I knew something was wrong.'

He sat on a breakfast stool and drank red wine while she grilled a steak, and it was only after he had eaten and some of the strain had cleared from his face that Marianne said, 'Why did you ask the builders to stop work, Rafe? I still don't understand.'

He drew her to her feet, wrapping her in his arms. 'This house is more to you than bricks and mortar,' he said softly. 'I understand that. And, as it stands now, all the changes have just made it better for family life and having friends to stay. I don't want it to become a hotel, Marianne.'

She stared at him. They hadn't discussed where they would live when they got married, there hadn't been time, but with the chain of hotels and all, she had assumed it would be America. Tentatively, she said, 'As a holiday home, you mean?'

'Not unless you'd prefer it that way.' He stroked her hair from her forehead, tracing a path down the side of her face with one finger. 'I'll have to talk to Dad, of course, and it would take some months to pull off, but I'm thinking of selling the business. We're fifty-fifty, Dad and I, but I can't see any objections from his quarter. He's made it clear he sees his life here from now on.'

Marianne nodded. She hadn't told Rafe about his father's proposal to Crystal, feeling it was the older couple's right to do it in their own way.

'But would you want to do that?' she said slowly. It would be a huge step for him to take.

'A few months ago, if anyone told me I would be thinking of settling in England I would have told them they were crazy,' he admitted softly. 'Now it's different. I'd like to buy a beach house in Malibu, though. I've got plenty of friends there and it would be a base when we visit my relatives. You'd like it, I promise. There are even those who say the Pacific rivals the Cornish sea,' he teased.

'Not you, I hope.'

'Never me.' He drew her into him, kissing her until she was breathless. 'Would you like our children to grow up at Seacrest?' he murmured against her mouth.

'You know I would.'

'Then that's settled.' He kissed her again. 'I might even come out of the hotel trade altogether. When we have kids I want to spend time with them, be there, you know?'

Marianne nodded. Yes, she knew. Andrew was a lovely man and he would be a wonderful father-in-law and grandfather, but the amount of time he had put into his business when Rafe was growing up had taken its toll on their relationship.

'Did I tell you I'm a qualified surveyor?' He smiled at her surprise. 'It seemed obvious in view of the hotel business when I was deciding what degree to take. And the beauty of it is, unlike some other professions, surveying knows no territorial bounds. I can practise my skills anywhere in the world. So don't worry, I won't become a couch potato when the business is sold.'

'I wouldn't mind if you do as long as it's my couch you're vegging on.'

He looked at her, all amusement gone. 'Always,' he said softly. 'Always.'

* * *

They were married exactly six weeks later at the little parish church in the village which was decked out for the harvest festival service the next day. In view of her parents' passing, Marianne had wanted a quiet ceremony with only Crystal and Andrew—who had tied the knot the week before at the local register office—and one or two very close friends present.

Rafe's closest friend—a tall blond Texan complete with stirrup-heeled, silver-toed boots and an accent so thick you could cut it with a knife—flew over to be his best man, bringing his small attractive wife and three blond children with him. Tom Blackthorn gave Marianne away and Gillian and Crystal cried all through the service.

Although the wedding was small, it was perfect. Marianne looked beautiful in a simple full-length gown of white silk, her hair threaded with tiny violet orchids which were reflected in the small posy she carried. Rafe cried unashamedly as she walked down the aisle towards him on Tom's arm.

Afterwards the little group went to the hotel overlooking the harbour for a wonderful evening meal in the small room Rafe had reserved, champagne flowing until the early hours. They had promised the rest of Rafe's friends and relations in America they would hold a big party in the States when they came back from their month's honeymoon in Bermuda, followed by another in England for Marianne's friends once they were home.

But now it was two o'clock in the morning and they had just arrived home at Seacrest, where they were staying for two days before departing for Bermuda. A round harvest moon bathed the mellow old house in moonlight as they stood on the doorstep, the taxi departing. In the distance, on the beach below the cliffs, the sea murmured its timeless call and the autumnal air carried the scent of the last of the roses blooming on the trellis attached to the house.

It was a beautiful night. Life was beautiful. Rafe looked up into the black velvet sky studded with stars and then lifted Marianne into his arms to carry her across the threshold. He had waited for this woman longer than he had waited for any other and he was glad of it. She was special. Their life together was going to be special and he would work every day to make it so. From being alone, he had been given a priceless gift of a woman he did not deserve to share his life. There was the hope of children, grandchildren, but even if this did not happen Marianne would be enough for him. 'Happy?' he whispered, stepping into the shadowed hall.

She brought his mouth down to hers in answer, her fingers fierce as they tangled in his hair. It started a chain reaction neither of them wanted to stop.

As he set her on her feet she clung to him and the fire inside him took over, the reality of the touch and taste and scent of her more intoxicating than any champagne. Helplessly he devoured her mouth, knowing this time he didn't have to stop. This time he could take her, she was his before God and man and the knowledge was heady.

Her body moved against his, as fluid and sweet as wine, and his hands found the zipper of her dress. As it pooled to white mist at her feet he saw she was wearing the scantiest of bra and panties, her sheer white stockings held up by some modern miracle his male mind didn't ponder. The need was raging, overpowering, taking over the control he had been master of for so long.

Her hands were feverishly undoing his shirt but, as they moved to the belt of his trousers, he stopped her. 'Not here,' he muttered hoarsely. 'And not like this. We're going to take our time, my love. I want my mouth here…and here…' His hands slid over her breasts and stomach, stopping at the warm feminine mound at the juncture of her thighs. 'I want to taste you, to make it last for ever. And the first time I have you will be in our bed.'

He lifted her into his arms again and held her high against his bare chest, his open shirt fluttering as he took the stairs two at a time. In their room they finished undressing each other and she was even more beautiful than he had dreamed, her silky honeyed skin, small pert breasts and long, long legs blowing his mind. He drew her down onto the huge soft bed they had chosen together, the scented cotton cool against his hot skin.

He was not going to rush this. Whatever it took, this was going to be a night they would remember for the rest of their lives. Damn it, he thought, they had waited for it long enough.

Gathering her against his body, he crushed her mouth possessively but almost immediately drew on the control which never failed. He began to kiss her face, her throat, her breasts with his lips and tongue before moving down on to her belly and then lower. He touched and tasted her delicately at first, giving her more and more until her hands were hot on his skin, her body molten as she writhed against him. She was moaning low in her throat but still he withheld what they both wanted until he could not wait one more moment.

He felt her stiffen for one brief second as he made her his but then she was moving under him again, her hands pulling him fiercely against her as she let her body tell him what she craved. And he was lost, a furnace of passion engulfing him as the last of his fragile control was burnt up in the glory that was her soft yielding body. An ecstasy that was mirrored on her face spiralled him higher and higher until the world was left behind and they both entered a place beyond time. He gave her his love, his body, his mind, his will, all self-preservation gone for ever. She held his heart in her small hands and always would.

It was very late when Marianne awoke the next morning. In the moment before she opened her eyes, she was aware of soft warmth and a pleasant all-over ache, and then bright daylight claimed her senses. Rafe was lying facing her, one strong, hard arm draped possessively over her middle. He was fast asleep, his long thick eyelashes resting on his cheekbones in a way that fascinated her. She let herself enjoy the wonder of drinking in the sight of him for long minutes, taking her time as she wandered over each feature, each inch of his face. He was beautiful, she thought breathlessly. So beautiful. His body, too. Last night in the moonlight she had seen how powerfully muscled he was and without an inch of surplus flesh.

The thought of their wedding night brought a sensuous heaviness to her limbs. In her naivety she had thought their coming together would be over once he had entered her and made her his, but he had spent all night until dawn broke showing her differently. He had been gentle and fierce, playful and dominant, lusty and loving. So many different depths to his loving. She stretched lazily, her eyes closing.

'Good morning, Mrs Steed.'

She opened her eyes to see Rafe regarding her with sleepy pleasure and, in spite of all the intimacies of the night before, she blushed as she said, 'Good morning.'

He drew her into him, kissing her thoroughly before he said with some satisfaction, 'You taste of champagne.'

'Well, don't expect that every morning,' she said breathlessly, amazed at how much she wanted him considering the hours of lovemaking they had indulged in.

'Why not?' He grinned at her, propping himself on one elbow and lightly tracing the line of her throat and collarbone. 'I think that's one habit we ought to adopt. Champagne for dinner every night if it has the sort of effect it did yesterday.'

She blushed again and he laughed out loud, pulling her on top of him as he said, 'Don't stop doing that, it's kinda cute.'

She tried to frown at him but it was difficult when his body was telling her he needed her every bit as much as she needed him.

They made love again, the sunlight bathing their bodies in a golden glow as they moved together in the sanctuary of their bed. Afterwards he lay stroking her hair and letting his fingers brush her cheeks for a moment or two before he said, 'What? What is it?'

'Nothing.' She hadn't known her thoughts were showing on her face.

'Marianne, we said no secrets.' He propped himself on his elbow, his blue eyes keen. 'What is it?'

'Those…those other women. They were experienced. They knew how to please you. I—'

He stopped her with one finger on her lips. 'Never, ever think that,' he murmured softly, his voice deep and more sincere than she had ever heard it. 'Last night was more beautiful than anything I have experienced before. You are my sun, moon and stars, my everything. Nothing else matters but you. I had never imagined before I met you that making love could be so consuming. I only have to touch you and I'm in heaven. It's never been like that before. Do you believe me?'

She stared at him, seeing the love. The last of her doubts fading way, she smiled. 'Yes,' she said. 'Yes, I believe you.'

'For richer, for poorer. In sickness and in health. Till death us do part. We're one, my love.'

And so it remained.

* * * * *

One

Hunter Cabot, Navy SEAL, had a healing bullet wound in his side, thirty days' leave and, apparently, a wife he'd never met.

On the drive into his hometown of Springville, California, he stopped for gas at Charlie Evans's service station. That's where the trouble started.

"Hunter! Man, it's good to see you! Margie didn't tell us you were coming home."

"Margie?" Hunter leaned back against the front fender of his black pickup truck and winced as his side gave a small twinge of pain. Silently then, he watched as the man he'd known since high school filled his tank.

Charlie grinned, shook his head and pumped gas. "Guess your wife was lookin' for a little 'alone' time with you, huh?"

"My—" Hunter couldn't even say the word. *Wife?* He didn't have a wife. "Look, Charlie..."

"Don't blame her, of course," his friend said with a wink as he finished up and put the gas cap back on. "You being gone all the time with the SEALs must be hard on the ol' love life."

He'd never had any complaints, Hunter thought, frowning at the man still talking a mile a minute. "What're you—"

"Bet Margie's anxious to see you. She told us all about that R and R trip you two took to Bali." Charlie's dark brown eyebrows lifted and wiggled.

"Charlie..."

"Hey, it's okay, you don't have to say a thing, man."

What the hell could he say? Hunter shook his head, paid for his gas and as he left, told himself Charlie was just losing it. Maybe the guy had been smelling gas fumes too long.

But as it turned out, it wasn't just Charlie. Stopped at a red light on Main Street, Hunter glanced out his window to smile at Mrs. Harker, his second-grade teacher who was now at least a hundred years old. In the middle of the crosswalk, the old lady stopped and shouted, "Hunter Cabot, you've got yourself a wonderful wife. I hope you appreciate her."

Scowling now, he only nodded at the old woman—the only teacher who'd ever scared the crap out of him. What the hell was going on here? Was everyone but him nuts?

His temper beginning to boil, he put up with a few more comments about his "wife" on the drive through town before finally pulling into the wide, circular drive leading to the Cabot mansion. Hunter didn't have a clue what was going on, but he planned to get to the bottom of it. Fast.

He grabbed his duffel bag, stalked into the house and paid no attention to the housekeeper, who ran at him, fluttering both hands. "Mr. Hunter!"

"Sorry, Sophie," he called out over his shoulder as he took the stairs two at a time. "Need a shower, then we'll talk."

He marched down the long, carpeted hallway to the

rooms that were always kept ready for him. In his suite, Hunter tossed the duffel down and stopped dead. The shower in his bathroom was running. His *wife?*

Anger and curiosity boiled in his gut, creating a churning mass that had him moving forward without even thinking about it. He opened the bathroom door to a wall of steam and the sound of a woman singing—off-key. Margie, no doubt.

Well, if she was his wife...Hunter walked across the room, yanked the shower door open and stared in at a curvy, naked, temptingly wet woman.

She whirled to face him, slapping her arms across her naked body while she gave a short, terrified scream.

Hunter smiled. "Hi, honey. I'm home."

* * * * *

Be sure to look for
AN OFFICER AND A MILLIONAIRE
by USA TODAY *bestselling author Maureen Child.*
Available January 2009 from Silhouette Desire.

HARLEQUIN *Presents*

EXCLUSIVELY HIS

Back in his bed—and he's better than ever!

Whether you shared his bed for one night or five
years, certain men are impossible to forget!
He might be your ex, but when you're back in his
bed, the passion is not just hot, it's scorching!

CLAIMED BY THE
ROGUE BILLIONAIRE
by **Trish Wylie**

Available January 2009
Book #2794

*Look for more Exclusively His novels
from Harlequin Presents in 2009!*

www.eHarlequin.com

HP12794R

HARLEQUIN *Presents*

Demure but defiant...
Can three international playboys
tame their disobedient brides?

Lynne Graham

presents

Virgin BRIDES ❤ *Arrogant* HUSBANDS

Proud, masculine and passionate, these men are used
to having it all. In stories filled with drama, desire
and secrets of the past, find out how these arrogant
husbands capture their hearts.

THE GREEK TYCOON'S DISOBEDIENT BRIDE
Available December 2008, Book #2779

THE RUTHLESS MAGNATE'S VIRGIN MISTRESS
Available January 2009, Book #2787

THE SPANISH BILLIONAIRE'S PREGNANT WIFE
Available February 2009, Book #2795

www.eHarlequin.com

HP12787

REQUEST YOUR FREE BOOKS!

2 FREE NOVELS PLUS 2 FREE GIFTS!

YES! Please send me 2 FREE Harlequin Presents® novels and my 2 FREE gifts (gifts are worth about $10). After receiving them, if I don't wish to receive any more books, I can return the shipping statement marked "cancel". If I don't cancel, I will receive 6 brand-new novels every month and be billed just $4.05 per book in the U.S. or $4.74 per book in Canada, plus 25¢ shipping and handling per book and applicable taxes, if any*. That's a savings of close to 15% off the cover price! I understand that accepting the 2 free books and gifts places me under no obligation to buy anything. I can always return a shipment and cancel at any time. Even if I never buy another book, the two free books and gifts are mine to keep forever.

106 HDN ERRW 306 HDN ERRL

Name	(PLEASE PRINT)	
Address		Apt. #
City	State/Prov.	Zip/Postal Code

Signature (if under 18, a parent or guardian must sign)

Mail to the **Harlequin Reader Service**:
IN U.S.A.: P.O. Box 1867, Buffalo, NY 14240-1867
IN CANADA: P.O. Box 609, Fort Erie, Ontario L2A 5X3

Not valid to current subscribers of Harlequin Presents books.

Want to try two free books from another line?
Call 1-800-873-8635 or visit www.morefreebooks.com.

* Terms and prices subject to change without notice. N.Y. residents add applicable sales tax. Canadian residents will be charged applicable provincial taxes and GST. Offer not valid in Quebec. This offer is limited to one order per household. All orders subject to approval. Credit or debit balances in a customer's account(s) may be offset by any other outstanding balance owed by or to the customer. Please allow 4 to 6 weeks for delivery. Offer available while quantities last.

Your Privacy: Harlequin Books is committed to protecting your privacy. Our Privacy Policy is available online at www.eHarlequin.com or upon request from the Reader Service. From time to time we make our lists of customers available to reputable third parties who may have a product or service of interest to you. If you would prefer we not share your name and address, please check here. ☐

HP08R

MISTRESS
TO A
MILLIONAIRE

She's his in the bedroom, but he can't buy her love…

Showered with diamonds,
draped in exquisite lingerie,
whisked around the world…
The ultimate fantasy becomes a reality
in
Sharon Kendrick's

BOUGHT FOR THE SICILIAN BILLIONAIRE'S BED

Available Janary 2009
Book #2789

Live the dream with more
Mistress to a Millionaire titles
by your favorite authors

Coming soon!

www.eHarlequin.com   HP12789

HIS VIRGIN MISTRESS

Bedded by command!

He's wealthy, commanding, with the self-assurance of a man who knows he has power. He's used to sophisticated, confident women who fit easily into his glamorous world.

She's an innocent virgin, inexperienced and awkward, yet to find a man worthy of her love.

Swept off her feet and into his bed, she'll be shown the most exquisite pleasure—and he'll demand she be his mistress!

Don't miss any of the fabulous stories this month in Presents EXTRA!

Available in January 2009

www.eHarlequin.com

HPE0109